MW00935408

Copyright 2014 J.

This book is a work of fiction. Any names or characters, any resemblance to actual events or locations is purely coincidental.

Cover

Cover design by Eisele Mountain Creations.

ISBN 13: 978-1500878214

ISBN-10: 1500878219

Dedication

To Carl and Marty – and to the New Year's tradition which started in Amherst. No matter where life takes us, New Year's Eve should always be celebrated with dear friends, champagne… and Cletus and the Klumps. No new year should ever be rung in without you two! You are our dearest friends; those time nor distance will ever change. I am a better person for knowing you.

To Dave, my biggest fan, my rock, and the love of my life.

And to the Most High who has put the dream in my heart, the opportunity in my path, and the joy in my soul.

I am truly blessed.

Holiday Wish

by

J.D. Wylde

Enjoy!
J.D. Wylde

Table of Contents

Chapter One

Chelsea Chathford wasn't an advocate of Cinderella fantasies, but she'd found herself stuck in one for the last year. Wishing on stars. Dreaming of a Prince Charming who wasn't always princely. Or charming. But with the New Year rapidly approaching, her fervent holiday wish was to have Vaughn Jennings, her Prince Charming of choice, naked.

Okay. Naked and an eager participant in whatever direction her fantasy took. Because that's what it was.

Fantasy.

It was on days like this, even standing amid sawdust, working with the best tools money could buy, that Chelsea really missed Cumberland, the small town she'd grown up in Harlan County, Kentucky. It was a long way from Harrington, North Carolina, where she worked for Jennings Restoration. It didn't matter she was doing what she'd trained to do. That she was recognized for her skills. And not lusted after for her breasts. When the end-of-year holidays loomed out in front of her, long and lonely, she got homesick.

Momma would be gone thirteen years this December. Papa was still alive, still living in Harlan County. He hadn't made it down to Harrington for Thanksgiving. She wouldn't be going home for Christmas. She'd be here, in Harrington, ringing in the New Year by herself.

That was really the problem.

She was alone. And she was tired of it.

She wanted a life shared with someone she loved. She wanted a husband. And since it didn't appear one was going to fall out of Santa's sleigh to land under her Christmas tree, she'd settle for a steady man in her life. But he had to love her. Accept her, too, exactly as she was.

No easy feat. There were five-feet-ten-and-a-half-inches of her. And a solid one-hundred and seventy pounds. Most men she looked in the eye. And the few interested ones she could look up to, well, they didn't know how to handle what she did.

She was a master carpenter.

Not the usual profession for a woman.

She clamped the piece of Kentucky cherry. Slowly ran an appreciative hand over the fine-grained wood she'd chosen to use for this reproduction. She reached for the gouge needed to make the dovetail joint.

It was in her papa's workshop in Cumberland, working by his side where she'd learned to be a carpenter. She'd been burying her grief at her momma's passing. He'd been teaching her a trade. One he'd hoped she'd use in Harlan.

The hum and whine of the state-of-the-art equipment in Vaughn Jennings' Harrington, North Carolina shop reminded her of how far she'd come. Going home every night to an empty apartment, loving a man who didn't love her back reminded her of how far she had yet to go.

It wasn't easy being a woman in a predominately male profession. It wasn't easy finding a man who'd understand her. And accept her. Work boots, chisels, and tomboy tendencies. Tool belt, jeans, and Jim Beam. She wouldn't change who she was to get a man. Or to keep one. She was done doing that. Had the emotional baggage stuffed down deep inside to prove it.

"Hey, Cha-Cha."

Chelsea lifted her head at the sound of her nickname. Everyone in the shop had one.

"You got that estimate for Hard-ass?" the latest office temp asked.

Even Vaughn, the owner of Jennings Restoration had one.

"You shouldn't call him that," she told the woman.

She got a shrug of indifference for her effort. "It's on the table." Chelsea jerked her head in direction.

Vaughn. Her heart threw itself into a tailspin. Her Prince Charming was her boss. She'd liked and respected the man from the start. For four years they'd built a friendship. But somehow, in the last year, with every moment they'd spent together, the like had deepened, and it had turned into the worst kind of love.

The fatal, one-sided kind.

And although she loved him, Vaughn only saw her as a

dedicated employee, a master carpenter he couldn't run his shop without. She sucked in a deep breath to dull the pain. Inhaled the scent of sawdust and varnish, and tried not to discern that she could still sniff out the man's cologne. He always smelled so good. "Enough," she chastised herself.

He had a stupid rule. One he followed like a religious zealot. And it was plastered on every wall in the shop. Big black letters on bright yellow metal.

No employee dating.

She wanted to take her frustration out on those ridiculous signs. She looked over to his office and she wanted to take her frustration out on him instead.

He was sitting at his desk, leaning over it. Intently concentrating on the pile of papers in front of him. All broad shoulders, dark hair, and brooding intensity. He did everything with intensity. And passion. And wasn't that just the most exciting thing ever? He was the James Bond of Harrington. Sexy. Mysterious. Dedicated. He knew their business like he'd been schooled at the master's feet. And he had a mystique about him that intrigued every woman he met. Chelsea knew. She'd been enraptured with him from the first moment they'd met. As had a half-dozen other women he'd dated over the years.

"What is your angle, Mister Garrett Vaughn Jennings?" No one knew much of his past, other than what was generically written in the business journal. "What secrets are you keeping close to your vest?" she whispered, as she tightened the clamp holding her newly glued joint. The man was thirty-years old.

Surely there had been *one* woman who'd been able to divert his attention from his stupid rule.

And damn, but didn't her foolish heart fill with hope she could be that woman. That she could be the one who'd capture his attention. And ultimately his love.

It would be the perfect holiday gift. An answer to her holiday wish.

She glanced up at the stupid yellow and black signs posted on every wall in the shop.

No employee dating.

And she sighed. It was the dumbest rule he'd ever come up with. She pushed her long blonde ponytail back over her shoulder. She'd never be the woman he loved. Because she worked for him. And he would never know her beyond the professional.

* * *

"Chelsea!" Lauren Foster-Forsythe called out as she left Vaughn's office. The former country music star had left him with a scowl on his face. She didn't usually have that effect on men.

"Losin' your touch?" Chelsea teased.

"Very funny," her friend replied, holding out a creamy ivory envelope. She shook it. "Take it."

"What is it?" Chelsea warily asked, holding a piece of rough cut walnut in front of her.

"Set your little board down and find out."

"It's not a *little board*." It was a gorgeous piece of rough cut she'd found in an old barn outside her hometown on her last visit. "And it will be a gorgeous piece of walnut when I'm done planing and sanding it." A perfect addition to one of the mantels in Bliss, the infamous house on the water, in Albemarle Sound. The house Lauren, as president of the Harrington House Historical Society, oversaw.

Chelsea was a history buff. She had the perfect job.

"I know it's not little. And you shouldn't be lifting it."

"I can lift it just fine." She was not petite. Not since she'd been ten.

"I'm sure you can. I wish I was in half as good a shape as you are."

Lauren Foster-Forsythe was cover-girl gorgeous. Even after giving birth.

"I think your boss should be out here doin' that for you."

Chelsea pointed a finger of warning. "You can stop your matchmaking right now. It's not gonna happen."

Vaughn Jennings was never going to see Chelsea as anything but an employee.

"Come on, Chels. Wouldn't it be fun to see all that lean muscle rippling?"

"Lauren."

"Get a glimpse of his ass when he bent down—"

"Will you stop? It still wouldn't matter."

"Sure it would."

"No, it wouldn't." She'd still be his employee. And short of quitting, that was how it was going to be. He was her boss.

And the initiator of the stupid-ass *No Employee Dating* rule.

"I've seen the rule enforced." It was why she was dragging her own lumber to the planer instead of having Josh do it for her. And why the shop was suffering through a temp invasion while Vaughn looked for another office assistant to replace Sarah. They'd been caught dating. And fired for it.

They were unemployed. But *blissfully* happy.

Maybe that was the trick.

"I should never have told you." If anything, it made her look pathetic. Chelsea turned. Reached for her protective eyewear.

"Chelsea." Lauren grabbed her arm, stopping her. "You said you'd think about it."

"I did. The answer is no." Attending an expensive fundraiser was way out of Chelsea's budget. "Hobnobbing with Harrington's elite, NASCAR's finest, and country music's superstars will only give me a bad case of hives."

"No, it won't. Come on, Chels. It's going to be fun. We've even got a celebrity bachelor auction planned."

Chelsea shook her head side to side.

"Come on," her friend pleaded.

"No. You'll have to hone your matchmaking skills on someone else." Chelsea's voice dropped to a whisper. "Vaughn and me?" She slowly shook her head side to side. "It isn't going to happen."

She needed this job. She wanted this job. Besides, she wasn't Vaughn's type. And she had a whole list of what she wasn't. Sophisticated. Beautiful. Or the three W's, as she liked to call them, worldly, wealthy, and working anywhere but here.

Chelsea schooled her features to hide her hope, and her vulnerability. It was tough being alone this time of year. Tougher when she loved someone who would never look beyond his stupid rule to really see her as anything more than an employee. Or to love her despite his stupid rule.

"Rules are made to be broken, you know."

"Not this one."

"Is it so wrong for me to want to see my best friend happy?"

Chelsea held a hand, palm out. "Do not go all girlie on me." And even though Chelsea succumbed to the same malady on occasion, she was, for the most part, a tomboy. Born and raised to run wild in Harlan County. And sadly, to lust after Garrett Vaughn Jennings in Harrington.

That was the way it was. The way it would always be.

"Come on, Chels. This is a chance for you to see him outside of here."

"I don't need to." She saw that dark hair and perpetual three-day scruff on his handsome face every night in her dreams. "Besides." She sucked in a deep breath. "Seeing him outside of here won't change his rule." It was the one thing

Vaughn refused to budge on. He was mulishly stubborn about it.

They'd spent plenty of late nights arguing over it when she fought to reinstate Josh and Sarah. She'd hadn't gone so far as to tell him his rule was dumb-ass stupid, but she'd come close. It didn't matter because Vaughn countered with, "*Rules are rules, Chels. And what good are they if they're not followed?*"

His rule was still dumb. *In her opinion.*

"He might change his mind, Chels. You know well as I do, Christmas is the season of miracles."

"Christmas will pass like it always does." With no miracle for Chelsea. No declaration of love from Vaughn. No rescinding of his stupid rule.

Lauren looked over her shoulder. "He's what? Six-foot five?"

"Will you stop?"

"I'm just making conversation." Lauren glanced into Vaughn's office, then back to Chelsea. "So what is he? Six-four? Six-five?"

"Six. Vaughn's six-foot six." The perfect height to make Chelsea feel feminine and sexy.

"Come to the fundraiser, Chels. Have some fun. Land yourself a date. Then reel him in and ring in the New Year with love."

"You are such a dreamer," Chelsea scoffed, ignoring the pinch in her heart. How many times had she dreamed that exact scenario? Only about a hundred different times. She sucked in a short breath. Let it out just as quickly. "Just because you have a fairytale romance, doesn't mean it's in the cards for everyone else. Thank you for the invite, but I can't attend."

And with her resolve shored up, and her foolish hope tucked away, Chelsea pushed her safety glasses back onto her face.

Chapter Two

"Rules are rules, Lauren." Garrett Vaughn Jennings the Third felt the need to point that out. "And they're not meant to be fun." They were meant to be learned, obeyed and lived by. "They're not made to be broken. Okay?"

He'd learned that lesson the hard way.

"Look." Lauren rubbed a wrinkle from her forehead. One he'd probably put there. "You agreed to be part of this fundraiser. For *Bliss.*"

Like he had to be reminded. Of his commitment. Or the infamous house on the water. Harrington House was Lauren's passion. She dedicated a large part of her life to preserving it.

He understood preservation.

"You agreed, Vaughn," she reminded him.

Like his word actually had value. And he didn't want to think too much about that small victory. "I did." He had. "But I didn't agree to be part of it looking like a redneck gigolo."

"You don't."

He snorted his opinion. "Who the hell thought this get-up

makes me look like a respectable owner of a restoration company?"

"With your charming personality, we had to pull out all the stops."

"I can be fun. Just like the next guy."

She was already shaking her head side to side. "No, you can't."

"Yes, I can," he stubbornly argued. Because he was a man. And that's what men did. But she was right. He wasn't fun. Or happy.

He hadn't been for a very long time.

He did a quick sweep of those gathered in the Harrington Civic Center where this dog and pony show was taking place. Laughter was in close competition with the music from a jazz band playing in one corner. The eligible bachelors were everywhere. Role playing in whatever costumes they'd been given, and obviously enjoying it as they "networked' with the professionals gathered. And they were moving and shaking it with the eligible women. Something he should be doing. And yet, he didn't. Had no desire to.

"I'm a businessman." He pulled at the shrink-wrapped plain white cotton adhering to his chest. "Who the hell thought a wife-beater spelled respectability, huh? Can you answer me that?"

"Look. I don't know what hills you come from."

He hailed from Savannah, Georgia where generation after generation of Jennings were born and bred. Had lived and flourished, too. Until, like the dinosaurs, they met an untimely extinction.

"But in these hills," she went on. "Women love wife-beaters. We find them sexy. And you," she pointed a finger at him to drive home her point. "You agreed to be part of the bachelor auction."

"I agreed." He pushed her finger aside. "When I thought I could wear the suit and tie I came in." For him, it projected respectability. Even if it was a prop, no better at instilling the falsehood than the outfit he was currently wearing.

Respectability isn't something you put on, Garrett. It's something that's earned.

Vaughn ignored the voice in his head. The one that sounded exactly like his father.

He could never make up for what he'd done to him.

Or to his grandfather's legacy.

He wondered why he was still trying.

"Look." Lauren squeezed the bridge of her nose with her fingers. "When the auction actually takes place, you'll be allowed to wear whatever you want. Okay? Does that make you happy?"

"No." It was Friday night. The night the numb-nuts left the shop early and Chelsea stayed late. He wanted to be back there. With her.

That would make him happy.

Just the two of them. Taking inventory. Looking over the next week's assignments. Talking to her. Spending time with her. Enjoying her company as much as he hoped she enjoyed his. Maybe even making her laugh.

Contrary to what Lauren thought, he did that. On occasion.

And Chelsea was smart. Nobody knew carpentry like she did. And she was unpretentiously beautiful. And sexy. God, she was hot. And—

He couldn't do anything but lust after her from afar because of his *No Employee Dating* rule.

He was the numb-nut.

"Bobby Wayne." Lauren snagged her husband, the retired NASCAR great, from the crush of people surrounding them.

"Hey, Sugar." The man in question wrapped his arms low around her waist and pulled her close. He lowered his head. Kissed his wife. Right there in front of everybody.

It was what Vaughn wanted to do. With Chelsea.

Declare his intentions and kiss her right there, in front of everybody, his rule – the one he lived by now – be damned. Would she show up tonight? He'd been looking for her in every blond-haired woman who'd come through the door.

"Talk some sense into him, okay?" Lauren told her husband as she slowly peeled herself out of his embrace.

"Why can't I be over there?" Vaughn pointed to a group of men in suits gathered around a baby grand piano. It was pansy-ass lounging against the big instrument, *in his opinion*, but it beat the hell out of the group of men in leather pants and nothing else hanging around a Harley in the other corner. Or the group of bare-chested men behind the bar wearing bowties, flipping glasses and juggling lemons like trained seals.

"Do you even play the piano?" Lauren wearily asked.

"No."

"Then you can't be a piano man. They're musicians. From Nashville, Vaughn." She bent down, retrieved the child-sized plastic hard hat he'd been given earlier. The one probably confiscated from Bobby Junior's toy chest. The one Vaughn had thought he'd stashed out of sight under a table nearby.

Lauren handed the hat to him. "Put this on. And you," she turned to Bobby Wayne. "I don't care what you have to do, or what you have to promise, but you get him smiling and friendly-like," she told her husband before she turned.

Bobby Wayne saluted his wife, watched as she was swallowed up by the huge crowd that had come out for tonight's festivities. He turned back to Vaughn. "So, what's it gonna take? You wanna date with Dana?"

Dana McMann was NASCAR's hottest, newest driver.

"No." She wasn't Vaughn's type. It appeared in the last year, he'd become very selective in who turned him on.

"Nobody turns down a chance with Dana. Are things not working right? You need a little blue pill?"

"No, I don't need a pill," Vaughn muttered. "I'm thirty. Not eighty. That's the last thing I need." He had no problem getting it up, especially when a certain statuesque blond of hourglass proportions was nearby.

"You wanna a contract to build the Bobby Wayne Forsythe Museum and Racing Annex at Bliss?"

"I wouldn't turn it down." Vaughn was a businessman. And the Forsythe's were his biggest client. The famous couple had awarded Vaughn's company the contract to restore Bliss, not once, but twice. They'd given him a golden opportunity when he'd needed it most. And Lauren, as overseer of Bliss was still sending projects his way.

Crap.

There was no getting out of this. He'd stand here like a trained seal.

Bobby Wayne patted Vaughn's stomach. "You're gonna do what Lauren wants, right?"

"I gave my word," he reminded his friend. And his word had to mean something.

If to no one else but Vaughn.

* * *

Vaughn did what was right. He quit whining. He even tried to play the part. But having been played once in his life – with disastrous results – he chose the straight-forward route. He stood with a smile on his face, or at least a baring of his teeth that, he hoped, resembled a smile.

Some guests talked. Some were actually interested in his business and what he did in spite of how he was dressed. Some walked by with a causal nod of their heads. Some lingered a while as their eyes roamed. But for the most part they kept a wide berth, which suited him fine. It gave him time to think.

Would Chelsea be here? Lauren was her friend. And if she did show up, would she bid in the auction?

What if she won him? It would sure as hell give him an out from underneath his stupid-ass rule. The one he couldn't really rescind without losing face. And respect – it was the only thing of value he had left.

And since the only way he'd have her was in a fantasy, he leaned against a wall nearby, and imagined. He'd pull her into his arms. Her height, her size, she'd fit perfect. His fingers would tease the curves of her ass as their bodies pressed close, touching in all the right places. His hardness pressing into her soft heat… Her breasts brushing against his chest… And their mouths, her plump lips made for kissing, he'd—

"Wow," a soft feminine voice shattered his daydream. "A penny for *your* thoughts."

Vaughn scowled at the woman who'd interrupted his fantasy.

She stepped closer. Her eyes smoldered with interest. The kind he should jump on.

"You've already got the tall, dark, and brooding part down pat. The scowl is really just overkill."

She wanted him. And he laughed at the absurdity of him not jumping on it.

"That's better." She smiled, completely misunderstanding.

He didn't correct her.

She offered her hand. "I'm Sydney Richards. And you're?"

"Garrett." Vaughn took her hand in his. "Garrett Vaughn Jennings the Third."

"Well…" Her smile grew. "It's a pleasure to meet you, Mister Garrett Vaughn Jennings the Third."

"Vaughn."

"Not Garrett?" she asked. Her interest in him wafted off her like the scent of the expensive perfume she wore.

"Not anymore," he found himself saying. He was no more Garrett the Third, than he was an young man from a wealthy family with a treasure-trove of old money and antiquities at his disposal. "Vaughn's good enough."

"Good?" Her eyes slowly traveled down over his body. And just as slowly back up. "The whole package looks pretty spectacular."

She wanted him. There was no misreading that.

And he couldn't have the woman he wanted, so, "Likewise," he found himself replying. He could play. It might have been a while since he had. One year *BC* to be exact – *Before Chelsea* – but he remembered how. And he wouldn't think too hard, or too much about what he was doing.

Or why.

Sydney Richards was beautiful. Close to his thirty years, give or take a couple. And, if he was a man on the make, he'd find her hotter than hell in the glittering dress she wore that plunged low in the front and equally low in the back. The scraps of fabric were held in place on her shoulders by tiny jeweled straps.

The dress easily cost a couple thousand dollars. The designer heels maybe another two or three grand. Diamonds glittered from her ear lobes.

She was no longer his type. But because he'd made a promise to the Forsythe's, and his word had to mean something, he said, "So, what do you do, Sydney Richards?"

"I'm an analyst. And," she turned her head to one side. Her hair fell over her shoulder. It was a seductive move. One he could jump on, but didn't. "I take it from your costume you're in the auction?"

"Unfortunately." He pulled on one leg of the sprayed-on jeans he wore.

Mid tug, her hand settled over his. High up on his thigh. Where it stayed. She leaned into him. Her breath warm against his chin. "Maybe for you it's unfortunate. But not for me."

She was a woman who was going after what she wanted.

She was exactly what he needed. With little effort on his part, he could have her. And then he could do her and keep doing her until he forgot all about his obsession with Chelsea.

And still he made no move.

She dropped her hand to her side. Her brow wrinkled as she tried to figure him out. "Are you in construction?"

"Restoration."

"Ahh. Preserving the past for the future."

Vaughn tried not to wince at her use of his grandfather's favorite saying.

There was no longer a Jennings Antiquities. Thanks to Vaughn, his grandfather's business, his father's livelihood, and Vaughn's future legacy was gone. That chapter forever closed by his selfish desires.

Sydney didn't give up. She stepped closer. Her tongue touched her lip as she slipped a finger under the cotton band of his wife-beater. Her fingers were cool as they slowly slid back and forth over his shoulder. "I look forward to bidding on you."

This was where he should say something, or do something.

She was giving him another chance.

Dating her would ease the frustration of seeing Chelsea every day and not being able to have her. It would—

Vaughn spotted a tall, curvy woman standing near the baby grand piano. Her long blond hair slid down her back nearly touching her ass. Her legs were long. Her heels high. And—

"Wow." Sydney tapped his chest, drawing his attention. "And here I actually thought I was exciting. Apparently I was wrong."

"You are… Exciting," Vaughn lied, yanking his eyes from the tall, leggy blond back to the woman in front of him. She was the woman he should be concentrating on. Not lusting after a woman he couldn't have.

The woman by the piano turned.

She wasn't Chelsea.

A volatile mix of emotion escaped Vaughn's chest with the hissing sigh of a deflated balloon.

It wasn't Chelsea. She wasn't here. And—

"There you go, thinking again." Sydney tapped his temple with her finger, before taking a step away from him. "And I'm pretty sure it's not about me."

He didn't owe her an explanation, but he found himself apologizing anyway. "I'm sorry. I just thought I recognized someone I work with."

He ignored the bitter taste the lie left in his mouth. Chelsea was so much more than someone he worked with. She'd been a hell of a lot more for over a year. He tamped down the guilt that somehow he was being disloyal to her by pretending interest in Sydney. He sighed. And he stepped back.

Because it always, *always* came back to Chelsea.

"Wow," Sydney softly replied, placing her palm over her chest. "That was potent."

She had no idea. And he didn't correct her misconception.

She slipped between his legs. And she stood close enough her hips nearly brushed against his groin. Her scent surrounded him.

And he tried. He really did. He looked into her eyes. He allowed his hands to go through the motions of sliding down over her back. Of resting low at her waist while hers slowly slid up over his biceps to rest on his shoulders. And he ignored the mental comparison he made of her to Chelsea. She cocked her hips nearly brushing against him. "You are good," she softly said.

The only thing *good* was their bodies didn't touch. Or she would know.

As much as he'd tried, he felt *nothing* for this gorgeous, sexy woman.

Nothing at all.

Chapter Three

"Gather round, boys!" Ricky Bobby called out, as he walked into the shop. It was Saturday, the morning after Lauren's fundraiser. "You, too, Cha-Cha," he said, as he walked by her worktable.

Chelsea fell into place behind Re-Pete.

"Check this out." He spread a copy of the local newspaper wide. With a finger he pointed to a picture. "That's Hard-Ass. As we've never seen him!"

Vaughn appeared to be in a line-up with a lot of other men. On a stage. A flock of women stood in front of them. Their arms high, their hands were full of... "Is that money?" she asked, craning her head over Beau's shoulder.

"Yes. Yes, it is," Re-Pete replied. Twice, as he was prone to do.

Beau cocked his head. "I thought *you* would have been there."

"Why would you think that?" she asked. A little too quickly. And a little too defensively.

Which, of course, snagged Ricky Bobby's attention. The

last thing she wanted was for any of the boys to realize what she thought she'd kept hidden this year. Her growing infatuation for Vaughn.

"You knew he was auctioned off last night."

"No. I didn't." Lauren had failed to mention that little tidbit.

"You knew about the fundraiser for the Harrington House."

"Everybody knows that." The goings-on at Bliss regularly made the paper. And in Lauren's defense, she had tried to connive Chelsea into attending. Maybe if her friend would have mentioned she was auctioning Vaughn off, she would have gone. And if she was still dreaming, as she obviously was, she'd have won him in the auction. He'd have no choice but to break his rule and take her out on date. And since this was a dream – a fantasy, actually– he'd have found her irresistible. And realized his stupid *No Employee Dating* rule was ridiculous. And—

Chelsea pushed out a breath. *She* was the one being ridiculous.

Vaughn was never going to change his rule. She was never going to be anything more than a valued employee. And any hopes, any dreams she might have of them, together—

She lifted her head. Ricky Bobby, Beau and Re-Pete were all staring at her. She tried to remember what they'd been talking about before her mind overdosed on fantasy. *Oh, yeah.* "I knew about the fundraiser."

"And you didn't attend?" Beau's eyes narrowed.

"And bid on Hard-Ass?" Ricky Bobby asked.

"No. I didn't attend. I didn't bid. And quit looking at me like that."

"I think the lady doth protest too much." Shake, who got his nickname because of his love of all works by William Shakespeare, added his two cents worth.

"I am not." Of course, she was. But she held her ground, sinking, as it was. With narrowed eyes, she stared them down. They looked away.

Ricky Bobby flipped a few pages to the society column's center spread. "Check out what we missed."

Apparently a lot.

She gazed at picture after picture of beautiful couples filling the Civic Center. Laughing, lifting their glasses high in toasts. Pictures of beautiful single women, dressed in semi-formal attire, coyly smiling at the handsome single bachelors, vying for their attention. And of course, more pictures of Bobby Wayne and five other men standing on the stage.

"*Woah-ho-ho*. Check her out." Shake was nearly drooling on a picture of one woman in particular.

And while the crew gossiped like old grandmas at the local Save-a-Lot, Chelsea slipped between Re-Pete and Beau to get a better look at the men gathered on stage.

One was dressed as a cowboy. Another dressed like a biker in head-to-toe leather. Beside him was another man dressed as an Indian. And she skipped over the rest of the lineup to Vaughn. Standing there. In skin-tight jeans. That left nothing to

33

her imagination. Or maybe she should say, it *confirmed* all her wild imaginings. And he was wearing a wife-beater tee shirt.

The breath left her lungs.

Mister By-the-book, Gotta-follow-the rules, wearing a wife-beater tee shirt? *Umm-mm.* It was her secret fantasy. And the skin-tight shirt outlined his pecs to perfection. The narrow straps of cotton showed off broad shoulders, which she always imaged he'd have. And muscled biceps, which she did know he had.

And that face. All angles and dark shadow of beard. And his eyes. Bright blue. Piercing and demanding at the same time. He wore no smile. Just a look of brooding intensity that had to have driven the women bidding on him absolutely wild. And he was wearing a child-sized yellow plastic hardhat, holding a huge sledgehammer.

He should look ridiculous.

Instead, he looked hot. I'll-do-you-right-here-and-ruin-you-for-any-other-man-for-the-rest-of-your-life. That kind of sizzling hot.

Chelsea squeezed her thighs together. Fanned her cheeks as a quiver of desire shot through her.

The photographer had caught the mirror ball casting bright shards of reflected light over the flock of women gathered close. The kind of woman Chelsea wasn't.

Rich and sophisticated. Beautiful and elegant.

And they were waving fisted handfuls of cash over their heads. The kind of money Chelsea didn't have. Even to bid on her dream man.

She looked away. To another picture. Six men on stage. Their arms raised in various angles, and with their bodies they were spelling out, "Y... M... C... A?" She looked at Ricky Bobby. "Vaughn was part of last night's entertainment?"

"Ye-ah!" Ricky Bobby was nearly giddy.

"Did you ever think you'd live long enough to see Hard-Ass prancing his badass around as one of *The Village People?*" Beau nearly giggled.

Chelsea's smile grew wider. "I wonder how Lauren made that happen."

"Forget how." Shake leaned over Chelsea's shoulder. "I wonder who bought him."

Chelsea smile vanished.

A woman would definitely have bid on him. Most likely *every* woman there, she miserably thought, as her eyes snagged on a picture of the man in question in a dignified suit and tie looking all corporate. And in the picture was that same unleashed intensity, that same *I'll-rock-your-world* assuredness projecting in his eyes and in his stance.

No woman would be able to resist that lure.

Chelsea's heart gave a painful squeeze in her chest.

Someone bought him. Someone would be going out on a date with him.

And it wouldn't be her.

It was the end of the first week in December. Another year

quickly winding down and she had spent it pining after a man who didn't see her as anything more than just another one of his employees.

Nothing special. Worse, *no one* special.

"Come on, come on. He's here!" Ricky Bobby pushed by her. "Let's go! Let's go!"

As if scrambling for a curtain call, the boys were pushing and shoving each other, creating a makeshift working man's chorus line across the shop. Right in front of Vaughn's office.

Ricky Bobby grabbed a wireless speaker from behind his work table. And a shopping bag. He tossed the bag to Shake. Punched buttons on his cell phone.

Chelsea put a hand out to Ricky Bobby. "What are you doing?"

"Let's go. Let's go! Get in line." Shake ordered, passing out props to each of the men. A motorcycle helmet. A child's Indian headdress. A tiny cowboy hat. A policeman's hat and—

"Handcuffs. Cool!" Michelangelo dangled them from his fingertips. "Can I have them for later?"

"Sure. Knock yourself out," Shake told him, handing off a combat helmet to Juice.

"Stop! What are you doing?" Chelsea stepped into the melee. "Vaughn isn't going to like—"

"Cha-Cha." Shake, who was built like a mountain, picked her up by her shoulders. With her toes dangling, he moved her off to one side. "We're just havin' a little fun. Don't worry."

The door to the shop opened. Vaughn walked in. Head down.

She pressed her palm to her chest. Right over her racing heart. It always did crazy, fluttery things when he was near.

Trumpets and horns sounded. Vintage disco music filled the air.

He jerked his head as the shop filled with the familiar sounds of the *Village People* singing *YMCA*. His dark brows drew together over his bright blue eyes.

Chelsea turned and stared, too.

The boys were clomping around the floor, wearing child-sized headdresses and tool belts. They were waving plastic guns and hardhats, doing a ridiculous impersonation of the iconic 70s group while lip-synching their signature song.

Vaughn stepped close to Chelsea. And it didn't matter what the others did.

When her heart slowed enough for her to catch a breath, she breathed deep. He smelled good. He always did. Like soap and aftershave, even though the dark stubble of beard on his face suggested he hadn't shaved in a couple days. But up his neck, there was a definite smoothness. And underneath his jaw, a line of demarcation. The kind only made by a razor.

He looked down at her. Smiled.

Her heart did another one of those fluttery flips in her chest. And when it settled a second time, she said, "You know they're imitating you."

"I am embarrassed to admit it." His smile grew. This time

reaching up into his eyes. They twinkled. And her breath caught. "But, yes, I do know."

"So you really?" she asked. And at his nod, she knew. She really should have taken Lauren up on her offer. Next time… She definitely would.

He leaned close. Bumped his shoulder against hers with easy familiarity. And he stayed there. In her space. His breath mingling with hers. Their arms touching. And further down… the heat of his body warming the side of her breast… her hip… her thigh.

It was ecstasy.

"Who knew the boys had such flash?" he asked. He didn't move. Didn't put any distance, professional or otherwise, between them. And the signals she was picking up. She couldn't decipher.

Their eyes connected and that simmering arc of awareness always humming between them, ignited. And it caught fire as it pulsed through her veins. Making her hot… Achy… And tuned in to his every nuance.

And he was studying her as closely as she was studying him.

Did he feel a tenth of what she felt? Would her wish for Christmas come true?

Her breasts grew heavy. Her breath, short. And the pulsing spot between her legs where all that exquisite energy was gathering, gaining momentum, grew moist.

And he was still looking at her. His breathing as rapid, as

shallow as hers.

"You hire only the best," she breathlessly told him, as she fingered the cuff of the long-sleeve, collared dress shirt he wore. His hands were big. His fingers long. And there was a dark sprinkling of hair near his wrist she wanted to stroke.

"And the most talented." His mouth curled into a slow, easy smile. His eyes lazily slid down her face and neck... her shoulders and arms... down to where her fingers were still fondling his sleeve.

He was her boss. And she shouldn't be feeling him up. That had to be an infraction of that damn rule of his. And yet he didn't pull away. And she didn't know what to think.

She dropped her hand. Curled her fingers into her palm to keep from reaching out and touching him the way she wanted to. Or taking the biggest risk of all, and just leaning in and kissing him. Right here. Right now.

She should turn her head. Pretend interest in the guys who were still dancing in front of his office. But she couldn't look away for long.

The top button of his shirt was open, as were the last two. The tails weren't tucked in. But they never were. He was easy, Sunday morning. And she wondered what he'd be like to wake up to on a Sunday morning. After a wild Saturday night rocking her world.

His beautiful blue eyes settled on her mouth. Where they stayed.

And she fought the most awful urge to lean into him. To shut her eyes. To lift her mouth to his and... Kiss him.

His eyes darkened. And all the clomping and stomping of work boots on concrete and vintage music faded away until it was just Vaughn… and her. And the air surrounding them, fueled by interest, sparked. Ignited. Swirling around them. Engulfing them. Cocooning them. And she could no more look away than she could stop her heart from beating. Or from wishing.

"I do have a thing for the best." His voice was rough-edged, erotically abrading her resolve the same way she knew his beard stubble would scrape against her inner thighs. More wet heat flooded her core.

He reached up. Gently tucked a lock of hair that had escaped her pony tail behind her ear. His fingers lingered. Stroking the sensitive spot right behind her lobe, and a floodtide of desire pooled deep inside her. His fingers curled. His knuckles gently stroked against her neck. And if anybody saw, she didn't care.

"You are the best," he softly told her.

Her breath backed up in her throat as his fingers slowly slid down to her collarbone, where they lingered. Stroking… and teasing.

Chelsea swallowed, uncertain what she should do. He'd never touched her. So boldly. So intimately. So… in front of everyone. She touched the tip of her tongue to moisten her suddenly dry lips.

"Don't tease." His thumb slowly slid up her neck. "I suffer enough already," he told her, with all the serious intensity that came natural to him. He dropped his hand. Slowly turned his head toward the guys.

Chelsea gripped the corner of her workstation to keep from melting into a gooey mess on the shop floor.

What did he mean, he suffered enough already? She pressed her palm over her thundering heart. While she reeled from Vaughn's sudden interest, he moved toward the chorus line blocking his office. While her world spun uncontrollably off its axis, his was everyday normal. Back to business.

"Very funny," he said to the guys who were still bumping and grinding like they were auditioning for *The Chippendales*. "Now get back to work."

"But Boss—"

"Back to work. I mean it," he said more forcefully.

Ricky Bobby turned off the music.

"At least tell us how much you went for," one of the other guys asked.

"No."

Vaughn was private. He never kissed and told. A trait she suddenly found very irritating.

"At least tell us who bought you," one of the other guys asked.

"No."

"*Come on.* Give us *something,*" the men whined.

And Chelsea wanted Vaughn to give *her* something, too. Starting with an explanation of what he'd meant earlier when he'd looked at her like he wanted to devour her. And when he'd told her not to tease him. That he suffered enough.

He lifted the tail of his shirt. Slipped his hand into his back pocket.

Her eyes settled on the perfection covered in denim. He pulled out a stack of cards. Held them up in his hand. "How 'bout I got seven requests for bids?"

Chelsea stepped closer.

Harrington, North Carolina had a lot of houses similar to Bliss. Not as extravagant, or maybe as old and storied with the kind of history Bliss had. Olivia Harrington's family built the house before the Civil War. There were still quite a number of stately homes, worthy of the kind of restoration Vaughn's company did. He was the best in Albemarle Sound.

"If we can get even three of these bids, we'll be busy for a good part of next year."

He turned back to Chelsea, cool-eyed, and all business. "I'm gonna need you to come with me on these."

And Chelsea's heart sank.

Gone was the heat of desire in his eyes. Gone was the raspy edge of want that had roughened his voice. Had she imagined it all? And then her eyes slid over to that stupid sign on the wall.

No employee dating.

And she knew she had. Because Vaughn Jennings would *never* ever consider breaking his cardinal rule.

Not even for Chelsea Chathford.

Chapter Four

No employee dating.

Vaughn stared at the stupid-ass sign mocking him on the wall when all he really wanted to do was stare at Chelsea. He'd positioned her workstation so he could see her from his desk.

No employee dating.

He'd made that stupid-ass rule when he'd come to Harrington from Savannah, still reeling from the catastrophe with Michelle and the disaster he'd made of the family business. The business his grandfather, Garrett Vaughn Jennings had started. The one he'd passed onto Garrett Vaughn Jennings the Second. The one his father had shared with Vaughn, fully intending he would be the third generation to run it.

Until Vaughn had destroyed it.

He'd been so sure of himself. So sure he knew more than the old man. He hadn't listened to his father's warnings when he'd made Michelle his personal assistant.

She'd assisted him all right.

She'd made herself indispensable. Both on the job. And in his bed. And he'd been so hungry for her, so blinded by his lust, he didn't see her sabotaging their company. Destroying their business, ruining his reputation.

And when he'd finally seen the irrefutable proof of her deceit with his own eyes, it had been too late to save the company. Too late to save his father. And way too late to save his own ass.

He'd lost everything.

When he'd relocated here to start over, he'd made the rule. And he'd plastered it all over the damn shop. He wasn't the hard-ass his employees thought.

The rule wasn't for them.

It was for him.

It was to keep *him* from repeating Savannah all over again.

He'd put the signs up in the shop five years ago when a curvaceous carpenter with the face of an angel and a centerfold body walked into his office looking for a job. She'd captivated him from the first moment he'd laid eyes on her. And not with just her expert knowledge and carpentry skills.

He'd never met a woman like her. Ever.

It was okay for the first few years. He'd ignored the desire building in his gut. He found comfort in other women. But Chelsea Chathford was a hard woman to ignore. Much as he tried to fight it, something happened last year. His interest in other women waned, and his interest in Chelsea had grown. It had turned to lust. And yeah, that's what he was calling it. And he had a hard-on for her ever since the turn of the New Year.

He couldn't stop thinking about her. He wanted to be with

her all the time.

And there was his dumb-ass stupid rule – his *No Employee Dating* rule— right between them.

He couldn't very well date her and say it was okay for the boss when he'd fired Sarah and Josh for the same offense. That was a lawsuit. He couldn't afford the damage to his business. The damage to his resurrected reputation, his name. And he couldn't very well take the damn signs down and say he'd changed his mind. He'd lose the respect of his employees. More important, Chelsea would lose their respect.

She was too special to him to let that happen.

So until he could figure out how the hell to get things changed, he was reduced to taking her along with him when he bid on jobs. It was lame-ass. He didn't need her there. He knew how to figure out estimates. Hell, he'd owned two companies. He knew how to formulate what it would take to price out a job and still make a profit.

He took Chelsea along with him because it gave him time alone with her. And if he took her to lunch or dinner afterward, well, he justified it by saying they had to eat.

He loved dinner with her.

Loved watching her relax after a hard day. The way she rolled the day's tension from her shoulders. The way she reached up and loosened the pony tail she always wore. The way she tossed her head as her thick blond hair fell around her beautiful face. He itched to run his fingers through that golden silk as it tumbled down her back like a waterfall. He itched to touch her curves, too. The swell of her breasts. Her hips. To wrap his hand around her calf and slowly slide his palm up her leg. Over her knee, then further and further up her thigh until—

He jerked forward in his chair. Leaned his elbows on his desk. Dropped his head into his hands. Hissed out a breath as his dick pressed hard against his fly.

"I have to find a way to change that damn rule."

And the sooner the better.

* * *

"You really think we'll get three of those bids?" Chelsea asked, as she rode with Vaughn through the downtown section of Harrington where Public Works employees were decorating street lamps with holly and pine garland.

"I could get them all," he confidently replied as he maneuvered the truck down the boulevard through afternoon traffic.

"That good last night, eh?" she teased, adjusting the heat in the truck. Winters were milder here in North Carolina compared to winters in the mountains of Kentucky. The highs were usually in the forties in December. This wasn't one of those days. It was cold out. Rain was mixing with a few flurries sputtering down from a foreboding gray sky, dark with the promise of more.

"Yeah, I was," Vaughn cockily replied. "But I'd rather have done it in a suit and tie." He shifted lanes. "There's rules, Chels."

She knew all about his rules.

"And you don't think Lauren's fundraiser followed any?"

Vaughn was a man who thrived on rules. Especially the ridiculous one he had posted on every wall in the shop. In her opinion, it was denying both of them what they truly wanted.

"Believe me. I would have rather sold them on my professionalism."

He didn't say *reputation*.

"I hated standing there like a side of beef. Being judged on what they saw, or what they thought they might get from me. Do you know how sexist that is?"

Chelsea laughed. "I think it was for fun, but, no, I don't have that problem. Men don't look at me like that." The guys she'd been involved with might have noticed her. But as they got more involved, their subtle suggestions and out-right requests for change were not because they thought her too sexy.

Vaughn pulled the truck off the side of the road. Stones hit the undercarriage as he brought it to a rocking stop. He tossed it into park.

Her brows drew together as she turned to stare at him.

He was gripping the steering wheel with fisted hands. Staring straight ahead. "Stop me, Chels. Before I cross a line." His jaw was clenched.

"Maybe I don't want you to stop. Maybe I want…"

He swung his head toward her. His look fierce. "I'm crossing *every* boundary here. *Every* damn rule I need to believe in. Follow. Every—"

"No." She slowly shook her head side to side. "You're not."

"I'm your boss."

He was so much more.

It was the season of miracles. She no longer wanted to wait on Fate. The worst she could lose was her heart, which he already had. Whether he wanted it, or not.

"When I came on board," she refused to say *when I came to work for you*. She did, but from the moment she'd stepped into his office for her interview, back when Jennings Restoration had been more dream than reality, "you told me," she softly reminded him. "I was your partner. That we were going to build this together."

Those had been his words. She was going to hold him to them.

"Chels." He breathed out her name.

Of course, he'd meant the company.

It had only been her, this many years later, who'd twisted them, building pipe dreams of love and forever after with him.

He squeezed his eyes shut. Just as quickly, snapped them back open. Churning bright blue orbs glared at her. "I'll be breaking *my* rule, Chels. Stop me. *Please*. Tell me, no."

Tension-filled seconds slowly ticked off as a volatile concoction of anger and anticipation mixed, detonating the explosive sexual chemistry charging the air surrounding them.

"No." She would not do as he asked. And she would not allow Fate to dangle what she wanted more than anything without reaching for it. "I won't. I can't," she added. Her voice was thick with the same desire pulsing through her. Pushing her to do crazy things. Like purposely trying to get him to break his cardinal rule so she could get what she wanted.

Conscience and desire dueled in his eyes.

Desire, the victor.

Warmth flooded her. Want and need sizzled along her nerve endings making her hot. And achy.

He reached out. Gently touched her jaw with his finger. Then just as slowly, brushed it against her bottom lip. "You are so… beautiful."

She had never thought herself like that.

"Sexy, too. And *that's* why I need you to stop me."

Her head slowly turned side to side. "I don't want to stop you."

She wanted him to throw his stupid *no employee dating* rule by the wayside. She wanted him to love her as much as she loved him.

He cussed under his breath. Reached for her. Cupped her face in his palms. Molded his mouth to hers.

She melted into his warmth. Grabbed his shoulders. Fisted his thick sweater in her hands as she opened her mouth to his questing tongue. She tasted. She teased. And nothing had ever tasted as good as he did. His tongue stroked against hers. She sucked it deep into her mouth. He growled out his pleasure as

51

he thrust and parried.

A tandem-axle dump truck rumbled by, blasting its air horn.

As quickly as Vaughn had consumed her, he released her. Pushed her back to her side of the truck. "That can't happen again." He heaved out a serrated breath. His chest rose and fell. "It can't," he roughly added, his voice hoarse.

More plea than declaration.

She didn't respond. If it was up to her, it *would* happen again. But she knew him. Rules were important to him. Especially that damn rule hanging on every wall in the shop.

The one he refused to break.

Even for her.

* * *

Vaughn held the door open for Chelsea. Followed her into Sarif's Seafood on the Sound. Slipping the head waiter a few bills ensured he got a private table with a great view. It was still in the main restaurant, but the tip would ensure no one sat near.

It was as good as Vaughn could have it and still be within bounds of his freakin' rule.

Christ. He'd kissed her.

They'd kissed three times this afternoon. Twice initiated by him. Once by her.

And now they were pretending like everything was the same as it had been yesterday. Except it wasn't. And it never would be again. His world was forever altered. Vividly recolored outside the lines.

He knew how she tasted. Knew she kindled the same feelings he did. And he knew there wasn't a damn thing he could do about them in the conceivable future without losing the respect of his other employees.

All because of his freakin' rule.

He wouldn't be getting any help from her. She'd made it abundantly clear how she felt. With few words and a whole lot of action, he knew exactly what she wanted.

Him.

Damn, if he didn't want to give her exactly what she wanted. But he couldn't. Not without breaking his own personal code. The one thing he'd sworn never to break.

What the hell was he going to do?

"Are you okay?" She draped her coat over her chair. Turned back to him. Eyes the color of the royal blue Henley she wore were doing a slow once over. "You've been pensive all afternoon."

"You think I'm *pensive?* Where in the hell did that come from?" He knew he was being an ass, taking his frustration out on her, but *Sweet Merciful Jesus,* she was the freakin' cause of it.

She didn't cower to his temper. Another thing he loved about her. "It's a stupid word, I'll grant you. But I thought it more diplomatic than sayin' you were *bitchy* or *brooding.*"

"You think me, a full grown man, *bitchy?*" The makings of a smile formed along the edges of his lips.

53

God. Even arguing, she made him happy. It was as simple – and complicated as that.

"Yes." She unrolled the linen napkin holding her silverware. Proceeded to polish each piece before placing them beside her plate. She was as meticulous as he was with detail.

And he could look at her all day. Especially today. The royal blue Henley she wore was the same color as her eyes. And it did amazing things to her perfect breasts, showcasing her every curve.

"Mister Jennings. Miss Chathford. Nice to see you both tonight."

Vaughn had brought them here enough times the wait staff knew their names.

"Good evening, Henry."

Chelsea remembered his name. Much to the waiter's delight.

"Ma'am." Henry sat leather-covered menus in front of each of them. "Can I get you something to drink?"

Chelsea smiled up at the waiter.

Vaughn loved her smile. And from the way Henry was looking at her, he liked it, too. How could she ever think men didn't look at her like she was hot?

"A drink would be nice. Bourbon, please. Jim Beam. On the rocks."

Vaughn liked a woman who liked a whiskey once in a while.

"Excellent." Henry turned to Vaughn. "Sir?"

"I'll suffer through the same."

"Suffer?" Chelsea arched an eyebrow. "You'll *suffer?"*

Vaughn found himself smiling at her as he told Henry, "Make mine neat." God, she made him happy.

"Very well, sir." Henry retreated to get their drinks.

"You know," Vaughn settled into his chair. "There is better whiskey than Jim Beam."

His grandfather had rows of very expensive blends sitting on glass shelves in his study. And Irish Crystal glasses specifically set out for it. As a kid, Vaughn would sneak into that room. Steal a few sips. He'd thought it awful back then. Funny how things change in life.

With her forearms resting on the table in front of her, she leaned closer. Enough to give him an unintentional but very enticing glimpse of cleavage from the opened buttons on her shirt. "Oh, really?"

And she was still staring at him. And he was still looking at her.

What the hell were they talking about? Oh, yeah... whiskey. "Yeah, there is," he told her. And if she called his bluff, she'd win, because right now he couldn't think about anything except how beautiful she was. And how he loved having all her attention focused solely on him.

Yeah, dad, I really am greedy and selfish.

"Well, I'm a born-and-raised Kentucky girl. And in the hills where I come from," and damn, if she didn't slip back into the mountain dialect. "If you're gonna *drank*, you best *drank* Jim Beam."

Henry returned with their whiskeys. He took their orders. While they waited for their food, they talked about everything but what was really looming large in the room.

Those three, sizzling hot kisses.

And this growing desire neither of them could ignore.

Henry brought their dinners. They ate pretty much in silence. He removed their plates, Vaughn settled the bill, and with a cup of coffee sitting untouched in front of him to delay the inevitable, his dark mood enveloped him.

"Vaughn." Chelsea leaned close. She wrapped her hand around his. Where it stayed.

He turned his hand, their palms touching. Laced his fingers with hers.

She didn't pull away, which only fueled the fire burning in his groin. "Is something wrong?" she quietly asked.

Everything was freakin' wrong, he wanted to yell. And in the same breath, he wanted to grab her. Toss her into his truck. Drive them back to his place and pick up where they'd left off three times earlier this afternoon. And then he wanted to push it further and harder and deeper until they both climaxed and got what they both wanted, consequences and rules be damned!

"We can go back to the Melbourne's, you know. You can give her a bid."

"I don't give a shit about the Melbourne's," he testily replied.

Did she not feel the same frustration he felt? The same helplessness at the futility of their situation?

She pulled her hand away.

He wanted to grab it back. Never let it go.

"I'm sorry," he said, with more gruff than remorse.

Her plump lips pressed together.

He squeezed the bridge of his nose with his fingers instead. Sucked in a sharp breath. Valiantly tried to resist the tempting woman inadvertently derailing all his good intentions. All his hard-learned plans.

"Vaughn?"

"Elizabeth Melbourne inherited that house, Chels. She means well with her grand ideas for restoring that old place. But even if I had lowballed the entire bid to below cost, she would still never be able to pay. She can't afford the place. She's gonna lose it before it has a chance to rot anymore around her."

"How do you know that?"

"I know when somebody's in over their head."

Like he was. Right now. He pushed back in his chair. Away from the all-consuming temptation sitting across from him.

Her blond brows drew together.

"Sometimes you have to know when you shouldn't go after something. When it's better to let things go. To move on." He stood. He tossed down a few more bills. "Because we don't always get what we want."

And wasn't the damn proof of that looking up at him?

Chapter Five

Chelsea reached for the old hand planer she'd brought with her from home. Yes, there were faster, more modern ways to plane the piece of pine she was working on, but she didn't want fast. Or modern. She wanted the repetitive motion, the monotony of routine that allowed her mind to wander.

And it naturally wandered to Vaughn.

A week had gone by since he'd kissed her. Seven days… and nothing. No repeat performances. No acknowledgement of what happened. Just him, ignoring her. Or him, sitting in his office, staring at her.

She didn't get it.

He'd kissed her. Yes, she'd kissed him back. She'd even initiated a kiss herself. But the day's final tally had been easy to count. Vaughn, two kisses; Chelsea, one. Add to her tally, one week of hurt.

She didn't understand.

She wiped away the accumulated curls of pine chips with her palm. Resumed her planing. And her pondering.

When his lips had touched hers, *slide… slide… swipe.* He'd

rocked her world. *Slide… slide… swipe.* The sizzle between them, explosive. *Slide.* Consuming. *Slide.* Volatile. *Swipe.* She paused. What would have happened if that truck hadn't blown its horn?

It didn't matter. Because for the last week, he pretended like nothing happened.

Worse, he pretended like *she* didn't exist.

She was hurt. Her ego bruised. Her feminine vanity, which she barely knew she had, much less recognized, was pricked. And now… Well, now she was just plain mad. She set the planer aside. With more force than necessary.

Pete looked up at her with concern. "Something wrong, Chelsea? Something—"

"Nothing's wrong," she growled out her frustration at him. She pushed out a huff of breath. "I'm sorry. I'm just tired," she lied. She wasn't tired. She was mad. And she was sad. Because as good as she thought those three kisses were, maybe they didn't even register on the Garrett Vaughn Jennings lust meter.

She grabbed an orbital sander. Moved it over the surface of the pine, grinding away the spurs and imperfections the same way she wished she could eliminate the spurs in her personal life.

She sat the sander aside. Ran a gentle hand over the board. "Five years." She allowed the warmth of the wood to seep into her palm. "I worked for you for five years." But last year, her feelings had changed. They'd grown deeper. More passionate. And his… She rubbed her hand over a knot in need of additional sanding. Like that knot, his feelings obviously hadn't changed.

What was she going to do?

She wouldn't be like her Aunt Gert. She'd lusted after Vernon Hindman for fifty years. Vernon owned the local fuel station in Cumberland. And every week, Aunt Gert dressed in her Sunday best to fuel up her old Buick. She'd pull into his station, all made up and full of hope. And Vernon would pump away and chatter with her while he checked her oil and cleaned her windshield. Complimenting her, telling her how pretty she was, how nice she looked. And Aunt Gert would drive away, head in the clouds for days.

She dressed in her Sunday best, too, putting a pot of soup on to cook and a fresh homemade loaf of bread to bake when Vernon brought propane for the stove. Or the home heating oil. She'd only buy a little at a time, so he had to stop by a lot. He'd come in for a cup of coffee and a meal while he topped off her tank.

Her aunt made Vernon pies and cookies every week, too. Dropped them off at his garage. The old coot gobbled them up, along with her aunt's affection, and Aunt Gert died, still hoping on her death bed Vernon would acknowledge his undying love. Instead, he'd brought his girlfriend to her aunt's funeral.

Chelsea slapped the board in frustration. "Damn." She didn't want to be a modern-day version of her aunt.

"Chelsea?" Pete was staring at her again. "Are—"

Her narrowed-eye glare stifled his question. Before he

asked it. Twice. As he was prone to do. When she had him duly subdued, she lifted the board to set it aside.

"Chels!"

Lauren Forsythe walked toward her. Looking very feminine. Wearing a pair of designer jeans, heeled boots, and a soft-looking sweater. Most likely cashmere. She tugged off her fur-trimmed leather gloves.

Chelsea sat the board back down on her worktable and greeted her friend.

"Where is Mister Garrett Vaughn Jennings the Third? I have a bone to pick with him." Lauren slapped her gloves against her thigh.

"He's..." *Avoiding me?* She couldn't say that. Not with Re-Pete nearby. "Out on a job," she said instead. Jobs she used to accompany him on, he was now taking Ricky Bobby. "Do you think Vaughn's gay?"

Chelsea rubbed her forehead, glad Lauren didn't respond. Garrett Vaughn Jennings the Third was *not* gay. He was... an idiot. He was an ass. He was a jerk. But he wasn't gay. She'd stake her official girl card on it.

"He's avoiding me." Lauren glared at his office. "The jerk's avoiding me."

Join the club, Chelsea wanted to say, but refrained. Re-Pete was still nearby. And there were those *No Employee Dating* signs still hanging on every wall in the shop mocking her. "Do you think kissing qualifies as dating?" Nothing about their relationship was normal. Maybe—

"He has a date with Sydney Richards," Lauren talked over her. "She won him in the auction. Did you know Vaughn was the highest bid-on bachelor?"

"No, I didn't. And thanks for telling me there was an auction."

Lauren's brow drew together. "I told you. I begged you to come."

Chelsea sighed. Waved a hand in front of her, pushing aside the words. And the feelings of regret. Her friend *had* told her, but she'd been so hell-bent on not attending, she'd failed to really listen.

Not that it would have made a difference.

Even if she would have gone, even if she would have withdrawn her life savings to secure the winning bid for a date with Vaughn, she was still his employee. And he still fervently followed that stupid-ass rule of his.

No employee dating.

God! She wanted to rip those signs down off the wall.

"Sydney has called him repeatedly. He's ignored all her calls."

"Maybe he's busy."

Kissing and ignoring her, *the rat.*

"That still isn't an excuse not to be polite and return a phone call. The woman paid good money for a date. And she wants it. Before the end of this month. I don't want to lose her donation – or any donation. Harrington House survives on them. I have so much more I want to do with Bliss. You know about the bed and breakfast."

Probably. But it was most likely another one of those things she hadn't really listened to.

"Donors as generous as those at that fundraiser are hard to come by. Needless to say, Mister Garrett Vaughn Jennings the Third is not going to ruin that by— Wait." Lauren squinted as she stared at Chelsea. "What did you say?"

"I said nothing." Nothing important anyway. It was *her* obsession. *Her* problem to resolve.

Lauren grabbed Chelsea's hand. Dragged her off to the side. "First, you asked me if I thought Vaughn was gay, which I don't. And then you said, *do you think kissing qualifies as dating?*"

Did her friend have to have a photographic memory? "I didn't say that."

"Yes, you did."

Chelsea squeezed her eyes shut, hoping to make Lauren disappear.

She didn't.

"Look. I didn't mean anything by it. I was just blathering."

The intensity in Lauren's gaze kicked up a notch and Chelsea wished for the hundredth time today that Vaughn had taken her along with him. This time for a totally different reason than picking up where they'd left off.

Lauren crossed her arms over her chest. "What's goin' on?"

Chelsea looked over at Pete's station. Thankfully he was gone, giving them a modicum of privacy. She stared down at her feet. And then at Lauren's. "Do you think I could wear boots like yours?" Instead of her work boots? And would anybody notice?

"Of course, you could." Lauren squeezed Chelsea's arm. "Spill."

"He kissed me, okay?"

Lauren didn't say anything.

Chelsea lifted her head.

"And?" Concern filled Lauren's voice. And her eyes.

"And..." Chelsea sighed. "Nothing," she softly added.

"What do you mean, *nothing?*"

"Oh, *jeez.* Do I have to spell it out?"

"Yes."

"I mean," Chelsea inhaled a deep breath. "He kissed me. And now..." She exhaled, allowing the pain making her throat tight to escape. "He won't even look at me." Her voice broke.

She hated that.

Lauren reached out. Sympathetically squeezed Chelsea's fingers. "There's gotta be a reason. An explanation."

"Yeah." Chelsea shrugged out of Lauren's grasp. "It's obvious. He didn't like it." He didn't feel the same desire she'd felt. God! She pushed a hand over her hair scraped back in a ponytail. This was awful. Even worse when she spoke it out loud.

Embarrassment burned her cheeks. How pathetic she must sound.

"There's an explanation, Chels. I've seen the way he looks at you."

Chelsea pulled the band from her hair. Gathered all the loose ends back into a pony tail. She lifted her chin. Inhaled a breath. "It's okay."

It wasn't. It was horrible. The worst kind of Christmas gift.

"This is all my fault. I shouldn't have pushed him into the auction. He didn't want to do it. But I insisted."

"No." Chelsea shook her head side to side. Unwilling to be deluded anymore today.

Lauren grabbed her hand. Squeezed it. "Let me have Bobby Wayne talk to him."

"No. *Please*. No." Chelsea loved Lauren, loved Bobby Wayne, too. But she drew the line on the former NASCAR great talking to Vaughn. Bobby Wayne was hardly an authority on love. Not with five marriages under his belt; two of them with Lauren.

"What will you do?" her friend quietly asked.

Chelsea lifted a shoulder. "I don't know." She wasn't going to spend another year loving a man who didn't love her. She wouldn't turn into her Aunt Gert.

Lauren lifted her chin. "I know what you're going to do."

"No." Chelsea attempted to stop her friend. An exercise in futility, she was certain.

"You're coming to the New Year's Eve Gala at the house."

"I don't know."

It surprised Chelsea she hadn't outright declined.

"You're coming. I insist."

The words to decline, to beg off eluded her.

"Trey Daniels will be there. So will Luke Branson. And Derek Holmes. Half of NASCAR is going to be there, too. And—"

Chelsea dropped her head back. "I'll come. Just stop the name dropping before I change my mind."

"You will?"

"Yes." She would. And she'd—

Lauren squealed. Grabbed Chelsea up into an exuberant hug. And jumped up and down, leaving Chelsea no choice but to clumsily bounce along with her. "I'm so glad! You won't be sorry. I just know you'll have a night to remember."

Chelsea extracted herself from her friend's embrace. "I'm not looking for a night to remember." Only a night where she wasn't alone, sitting in front of her television, watching half of Hollywood welcome in the New Year in Times Square.

Her friend's eyes twinkled with excitement. "I'll personally introduce you to Luke Branson."

"Country music's hottest heartthrob? No thank you."

"Chels. I'm not suggesting you hook up with Luke. Or Trey. I'm just suggesting you meet someone. Enjoy their company for a few hours. Ring in the new year with them, if you want. Just don't spend New Year's Eve at home on the couch with Ryan Seacrest. Unless you actually have Ryan on your couch."

Lauren dipped her head. Stuffed her hand into her purse. She pulled out a creamy ivory vellum envelope. Handed it to Chelsea. "Here."

It was an invitation to the ball.

Her Cinderella moment.

This time she wouldn't refuse it. She held the envelope like a magic lamp. She was really going to do this. She was going to the ball. And she was going to go with her mind open to new possibilities. And—

"You'll come?" Lauren softly asked. "You'll really come?"

She looked at her friend. "I'll be there."

Lauren pressed both her hands together in front of her. Excitement propelled her up on her toes.

"No. Don't," Chelsea warned. "We aren't school girls getting asked to our first dance."

"You're right." Lauren assumed the regal pose Chelsea would expect from the president of the Harrington House Historical Society. That was until she dropped her head back and shook it. A veil of dark waves cascaded down her back. She pumped her fists up over her head in victory before grabbing Chelsea's forearms and squeezing. "We are going to have *so much fun*, Chels! We'll have manicures. And pedicures."

"No. We won't." She didn't do nails. Plain and clipped

short were fine. And the nail polish she wore on her toes, she could do herself, *thank you, very much.*

"We'll have our makeup done."

"No."

"Hair? Come on. At least hair."

"No," Chelsea replied, keeping it real. Much as she wanted a fairy tale ending, she wasn't Cinderella. And Lauren was her friend, not her fairy godmother.

"We'll go shoe shopping. You have to at least go shoe shopping."

"No! And stop. *Please.*"

"Why?"

"Because you're going all girly on me."

"Oh. Sorry. I didn't realize that wasn't allowed." Lauren had been after Chelsea since the second restoration of Bliss to go out with her on a girl's shopping day.

Chelsea always refused. What did she need dresses and heels taking up space in her closet when her work uniform consisted of work boots, jeans, tee shirts, and Henleys? "I have a dress." Three in the back of her closet. "I have shoes. I know how to do my own hair." And makeup… Well, she wasn't going to the ball to meet a man.

She was going to forget one.

"You sure?"

"Yeah, I'm sure."

"Oh! I almost forgot." Lauren dipped her head. Her hands were jammed back into her purse and Chelsea allowed the excitement to build at what her friend might have forgotten.

Lauren dropped a key into Chelsea's hand.

"What's this?"

"It's a key. To a room. At Bliss."

Chelsea handed it back.

Of course, Lauren refused it. "I want you to spend the night."

"You know I love history." That she'd get to spend the night in that house was a gift she'd never expected. "But..." Her eyes narrowed. "If you're back to playing matchmaker—"

"I'm not." Lauren crossed her finger over her heart. "If you hook up with someone, it will be all on your own."

That wasn't going to happen. "So why do I need a key then? To a room?"

"You mean besides the obvious?"

"I'm not hooking up." With anyone. And that was the sad truth.

"I have plans to turn the unrestored wing into a bed and breakfast. It's all still in the beginning stages. Bobby Wayne and I have a room. You'll have a room. Everyone involved in what will be the construction, restoration, and creation of the bed and breakfast will have a room."

Which meant Vaughn would have one, too.

For him and... Sydney Richards? God! The thought

sucker-punched her heart. She rubbed her fingers over the sore spot.

"I want us all to spend a night there. And after the holidays, we'll get together and discuss and see if this is even a viable project to pursue."

"But you're already pursuing it. Doesn't that make it a given?" Her friend was a fierce protector of the stately old mansion. Even though Lauren was not a blood relative, Olivia Harrington would be proud to have Lauren Forsythe overseeing the old homestead.

"Opening the wing up as a bed and breakfast, renting out rooms would make Bliss more solvent. And less dependent on the charity of others. But it's far from a done deal. I have miles of red tape to step through – with the Harrington House Historical Society, the Harrington City Counsel, the planning commission, the municipality. I need to know it's feasible before I start."

"You don't need me. You'll have Vaughn there." Reluctantly, she handed back the key.

Again, her friend refused it. "Chelsea. Vaughn might own this place, but you're the heart and soul of it. Bliss would never have been restored to its grandeur if it weren't for you. You're like the wood whisperer."

"Wood whisperer?" Was her friend serious?

"I swear you can channel Olivia Harrington's wishes just by running a palm over that old woodwork. I need you there. I value your opinion. Your talent and your insight." She put her hands up in front of her. "More, I value your friendship. I'm not trying to fix you up. Or set you up. Okay?"

"All right," Chelsea squeezed the old key tight between her fingers. "I'll stay."

And maybe for the first time since the disaster of those kisses one week ago, Chelsea was actually looking forward to the holidays.

And some holiday bliss.

Chapter Six

Walking with his trademark *Hard-Ass* glare firmly adhered to his face, Vaughn strode through his shop. He exhaled a breath of relief entering his office. No one had stopped him. He walked around his desk. Fell into his chair and dropped his head into his hands. He massaged his temples where the mother of all headaches was forming.

What the hell had ever made him think taking Ricky Bobby out with him on job estimates was a good idea?

Probably the same stupid-ass part of his brain that thought by avoiding Chelsea all day he would think about her less – or possibly even forget about his attraction to her.

Fat chance of that.

She was in his heart. And, *dammit!* He knew his condition had morphed into a terminal case of lust. And yes, that's what he was calling it. *Lust.* And *terminal.* He didn't see any freakin' way for him to have what he really wanted, which was her.

"Shit." He pulled his head out of his hands. Picked up the stack of messages Tanya, his latest temp, had left on his desk. Most of them were from Sydney Richards. The woman who'd won him in Lauren's auction.

He tossed the messages aside. He didn't want to think about Sydney. Or Lauren. Or his obligation to both of them. Or Chelsea. He lifted his head. To her station. He let out a sigh of relief. She wasn't there. He could think better without her distraction.

Yeah, right. She might not be there. But it didn't matter. He could think of no one else. Despite the pile of messages on his desk from the woman who could eliminate this whole mess he'd somehow gotten himself into – if he'd just call her.

Except he wasn't interested in her.

He wanted Chelsea. It was as simple – and complicated as that.

Lauren stepped into his office as Chelsea walked back to her station.

"What do you want?" He wasn't sorry for his tone. He didn't want to deal with her right now.

She didn't seem to mind his abruptness. "I see you've recovered from the other night."

"I have." Vaughn tried to be a little more civil. She was his biggest client.

"So you're none the worse for wear?"

"I'm good." He wasn't. But she didn't need to know that.

Lauren stepped closer to his desk. Her voice was unusually quiet when she said, "Vaughn. You have to call Sydney."

"I know." He was a man of his word. When he was given responsibility to do something, he did it. At least for the last five years, that had been his sole focus and intent.

"This year. And the sooner," she quickly glanced over her shoulder. "The better."

"I know. And I will." The timing couldn't suck worse. *In his opinion.* "I gave you my word." And he would do as he said.

It was better to call Sydney than try to pursue a relationship with Chelsea.

And when he should feel peace with his decision, unrest stirred in his soul. Discontent thrummed through his veins. When he should feel excitement at the prospect of a date – a chance at a relationship with a beautiful, successful woman who really seemed to desire him, well, all Vaughn could think about were a couple explosive kisses with a woman he couldn't have.

"I know you gave me your word. And I appreciate you participating. I do. But—"

"I said I'd do it." And he would. He was a man of his word. At least he was trying to be.

"It wasn't so bad, was it?" She looked as troubled as he felt. "It was meant to have fun— I never," she inhaled a quick breath. "I never meant for anyone to get hurt." And she chanced another quick peek over her shoulder. Toward Chelsea's station.

"Do we really have to talk about this?" He didn't want to. Not with Chelsea so close, so able to hear their conversation.

"You're right." That Lauren readily agreed with him made him uneasy. How much did she know? "So you had a good time?" Her voice turned quiet. "I mean besides… Despite…"

He pulled his gaze from Chelsea.

"I got some leads for work from it. Some are even promising."

Lauren exhaled a breath. "Good. I'm glad. And thank you, again, Vaughn. Before I forget..." She slipped her hand into her bag. "I have something for you."

At this moment, he wanted nothing from Lauren Foster-Forsythe.

She slipped an envelope onto his desk.

"What's that?" he warily asked.

"An invitation to the New Year's Eve Gala at Bliss."

She glanced over her shoulder to Chelsea, then quickly back to him. "Maybe you could bring someone?"

"Maybe." He wasn't committing to anything. Agreeing to Lauren's wishes is what had landed him in this mess in the first place.

"Special?" she went on. Again she looked over her shoulder.

Vaughn's brows drew together. Did she know his feelings for Chelsea? Had he been that transparent? Or—

"Are you matchmaking?" he straight-out asked. "Because—"

"No. *No*," she quickly replied. Heat colored her cheeks. "I look forward to seeing you there."

Vaughn nodded his head.

"And thank you again, Vaughn."

"You're welcome."

"Bring someone… special," she added, before turning to leave. At the door, she paused. She looked over her shoulder. "You won't forget to…"

He picked up the phone. He would do as he'd promised. He'd be responsible for his actions. "I'll call Sydney. Right now."

Lauren nodded. With her head down, she quickly left the shop.

Vaughn dropped the phone back onto the cradle without making the call. He picked up the invitation instead. Would his men care if he walked out to Chelsea's workstation and asked her to attend with him? Would she care? She had as much invested in what the men thought, as he. Maybe more. She was a woman trying to be respected in a predominately male profession.

But would she go out with him? If he straight-out asked her?

She'd kissed him. He'd kissed her. They had chemistry. Hell, his lips still burned from the contact. And his dick, well—

"I see you got an invite, too."

Chelsea stood in his doorway, looking windblown and disheveled. The unusual bitter weather outside had colored her cheeks. The wind had tugged strands of her blond hair from the ponytail she always wore. She looked cold. And hot at the same time.

Opportunity was here. Right here in this room. Teasing him. His heart beat fast at the thought. Could he just boldly go for what he wanted and who cared of the consequences?

No. He couldn't. And not because of the voice of contention in his head. The one that had followed him from Savannah. He couldn't do that to her. Because she was *special*. She deserved a man who could commit totally to her. And he still had unfinished business with Sydney Richards. Yes, it was just a date – one night out of his life, but it was still an obligation. Something Vaughn had to take care of before he was free to pursue Chelsea.

And yes, he was going to pursue her. Somehow in the New Year, he'd find a way to keep his employees' respect for him – and her – and still have her in his life.

She was still looking at him. Still waiting for a reply.

"Yeah," he managed to say. "You?"

"Yeah," she softly replied.

It was the most they'd talked all week.

God, he missed their talking. He missed the time they spent together. He missed her.

He wished he'd never agreed to be part of that damn bachelor auction.

She inhaled a breath. One that did amazing things to the fit of her Henley. She had the most amazing breasts he'd ever seen. "Well…" She let the breath out just as slow. And the attraction, a life force of its own, sizzled all around them.

He was an idiot. His father was dead. The family business

gone. All Vaughn had was what was here. And she was everything he ever wanted. And still he couldn't shake free of the ghosts that taunted him; that haunted his every move, his every decision.

She turned to leave.

"You going?" he found himself asking. He stood. Wanting to prolong their time together. Even if it was making stupid conversation with her from across his office.

She turned back. Looked up at him. He could drown in her beautiful blue eyes and die happy. She cocked her head to one side. Her thick golden ponytail slid to one side to fall over her shoulder. He wanted to wrap his hand around it. Pull her close. Press his mouth to hers and kiss her as he pushed deep inside her.

"To the party?" she asked.

"Yeah," he managed to say. He wanted to end this bump and grind. This attack and retreat. He wanted it done. Over with. He wanted to ask her to go to the New Year's Eve Gala with him. And *dammit!* He was going to do it.

"Chels—"

Tanya burst into his office juggling a messy armful of manila folders.

Vaughn cussed.

"Here are the files you asked for. I couldn't find them earlier. I'm still not real clear on how you— Oh!" She stopped near his desk. "I am *so* sorry." Embarrassed heat turned her face red. She back-peddled, nearly stumbling over her feet. "I

79

didn't realize— that you— That—"

"It's okay." Chelsea took charge of the situation. Like she always did. She put a reassuring hand out, bringing calm to the storm. "We were just talking. Please." She motioned for his latest temp to venture closer.

The woman took two hesitant steps. Looked up at him and with a hiccup of distress, tossed the files toward his desk before running out the door.

He cussed again as he jockeyed the teetering stack.

"How's she working out?"

"She's not." He'd made a big mistake going all hard-ass on his former office assistant and her boyfriend. "I don't ask for much, you know? Just put the bills that need to be paid on the top. The jobs that need my approval next, and—"

Chelsea stepped closer. Her scent surrounded him. She took the files from him. Methodically she opened each folder. She jogged the papers. She straightened the clips.

He loved her hands. Her long fingers with the short nails. Her touch, sure and gentle at the same time. He wanted her to touch him that same way.

She rearranged the contents, putting everything in the order he liked. "There."

She knew him better than he knew himself.

"You know," she sat the neat stack in front of him. "You could hire Sarah back."

"It's not that easy." He pushed out a breath of frustration.

For his aroused state. For his inability to somehow do something as simple as asking the woman he was crazy about to spend New Year's Eve with him because he'd allowed another woman to lead him around. And he was frustrated for the mess he'd made of his office by firing a woman whose only indiscretion had been falling in love with someone in his shop.

Just like he had.

Karma and Fate were surely laughing their asses off at his expense.

"Yes, it is, Vaughn. It's all very simple. Sarah and Josh…" She inhaled a breath. "You… and me…" She lifted her eyes to his. The sapphire blue of her irises turned molten. And the air around them grew heavy. A turbulent mix of excitement and frustration. "We're not hurting anything. Why can't you see that?"

"It isn't about *seeing*," he growled. It was about making up for past sins. It was about seeking forgiveness he was never going to get.

"Take the signs down," she slowly told him. "Make everyone happy."

And much as he wanted to do exactly as she'd requested, "I can't," he said.

"Yes, you can. Just take them down, Vaughn."

"I can't," he ground out. She didn't get it. And she never would.

Her brows drew together. "Yes, you can. Just call Sarah. Call Josh."

"It's not that simple, Chels."

"It could be. Take the signs down. And apologize."

"It's more than just damn apologizing, okay?" And his voice rose, along with his anger.

"Of course, it is. Offer them their jobs back. Take the damn signs down." Frustration and passion filled her voice. "Let everyone have what they want."

"Jee-suz," he yelled, his temper breaking free. "If it were that freakin' easy, don't you think I would have done it? Give me a little credit for intelligence!" Those wild, hot kisses were smoldering between them, mixing with everything he wanted. Namely, her.

"It is that easy."

And she made it all sound so freakin' easy. Like he could have everything he wanted by just doing as she said. He rubbed his palms over his cheeks, barely leashing his rage. "If only it were that easy, Chels. But it's not."

She'd never understand.

Determined to have her way, she leaned over his desk. Her lips close enough to kiss. "Tell me why it's not."

If only he could. But he couldn't put into words what he'd done. The havoc he'd caused. The lives he'd ruined. The dreams he'd decimated. All because he'd gotten involved with a woman at work.

"Tell me." Her voice rose in persistence. And exasperation.

And the words that would explain, and condemn him,

were stuck in his throat. And he was too much of a coward to say them. To have her see him for the self-serving bastard he was. And it wouldn't matter he'd done penance for that damn transgression for five long years. In the end he'd lose what mattered most. Her.

And her respect for him.

Suddenly it was all too much. His temper erupted. With one hand he cleared his desk. Papers flew like confetti. The carefully ordered files collateral damage of his rage. His chair banged off the wall as he stood. "It's not easy. And, *dammit!*" he spit out, leaning over his desk to get in her face. "Respect me enough not to ask!"

She leaned closer, claiming the remaining real estate between them until she was nearly nose to nose with him. Hostility and frustration, an angry toxic mix swirled around them. "Care enough, about *me*." Her finger speared her chest. "To tell me! But you don't, do you?"

If she only knew.

How damn much he did care. And how twisted up inside he was. Trying to make up for something he could never fix. Trying to stay away from something he wanted more than he wanted his next breath.

Her chest heaved. His gut twisted. And the words to tell her how he felt at war with his need to prove to a dead man he wasn't a disgrace. That he wasn't—

She pushed back. Away from him. She blinked her eyes. Her own emotions getting the better of her. And he wanted to kick his own ass for making her cry.

"Chels. I—" He reached a hand out to touch her. To pull her close, his stupid-ass rule be damned.

She stepped back. Out of his reach. Regally lifted her head. "I've been your employee for five years."

"Chels—" She was so much more than that. And he was an ass for letting her think different.

"No. You let me finish." She talked over him. "I think," she impatiently swiped a hand under her eye. "I've been your friend for just as long."

"You're more than a friend. And you damn well know it." Three explosive kisses in his truck confirmed that.

"Oh, yeah?" she challenged, her blue eyes glittering. "Prove it."

All it would take was his mouth touching hers again. And in seconds of that contact, he'd be dragging her over the desk, having her in his arms. Where he wanted her. And he wouldn't let go until she knew exactly what she was to him. But—

"You can't." She crossed her arms over her gorgeous breasts. "You can't do it."

He pinched the bridge of his nose. "Chels—"

"Excuse me, Vaughn?"

"*Dammit!*" Vaughn cussed. "What?"

Tanya's poked her head around his office door. "I'm very, very sorry to bother you. But there's a customer. In the lobby to see you," she quickly added, before shutting the door.

Chelsea huffed out a sigh. Pushed away from his desk. "I'll

let you go."

She said the words with such finality in her voice.

"Chels." He put a hand out. So afraid he was losing her before he ever had her. "Chels, stop. Whoever is out there can wait."

"No."

"Chels—" He stepped closer. Stole a touch, a brush of his fingers against her collar bone.

She put up a hand, pushing his aside. "I'll let you get back to your... *work.*" And before he could stop her, tell her what she wanted to hear, or show her, she turned away from him, retreating to the back of the shop.

Leaving Vaughn with his secrets intact; his heart torn with yearning, and his soul mired in a restless hell.

Chapter Seven

Her temper cooled, but the invitation was still burning a hole in Chelsea's pocket. She should take it home, set it on the counter, and figure out what she was going to wear to such a dressy affair. She shouldn't be thinking of picking it up and going another round with Vaughn.

She wasn't Cinderella. He wasn't Prince Charming. And her happy ever after ending wasn't waiting when the clock struck midnight.

Vaughn wasn't going to change his stupid rule. And he wasn't going to explain why it was so important to him. Yet even knowing that, it didn't change the fact she still wanted him. Anyway she could have him. And having him at the New Year's Eve Gala would be a holiday wish come true.

Go home.

Ignoring the voice of reason, she picked up the envelope. Tapped it against her finger. Mentally weighed the possibilities. He could say *no*. He could remind her once again of his stupid rule. Worse, he could tell her that although they'd kissed, it hadn't been *that* remarkable.

"The worst that could happen is you, sitting here

wondering. Doing nothing."

Tanya was gone. The customer, too. She'd seen their cars leave. She'd dilly-dallied in the warehouse long enough the shop was now empty. The guys had all gone home. After today, the shop was closed for the rest of the year for inventory and maintenance. Vaughn was still out in the lobby. She could see the beam of light shining under the closed door in the rear of his office.

She could march out there. Say what she wanted to say. Nobody would be there to witness her humiliation. And she'd know, once and for all, where she stood with the man.

She grabbed her invite. Before she lost her nerve, she marched through his office to the door leading to the lobby. Her hand hovered over the doorknob. A foreboding uncertainty stirring in her soul.

Go home. Put this craziness on the back burner, her conscience advised. But did she want to ring in another year not knowing? "No," she whispered, shaking off the uncertainty. She turned the knob. With a quick inhaled breath, she opened the door. Before she lost her nerve, she blurted out, "Vaughn, will you go to the—"

The words dried up. Along with any hope.

He was there.

Standing in the lobby.

He wasn't alone.

He jerked back. Away from his guest.

"Chels."

He looked startled... Surprised... And guilty. So very, very guilty.

"I'm sorry." She backed away from what she was seeing. Stumbling on her work boots in the process. "I didn't realize you had... company."

The woman keeping Vaughn *company* was gorgeous. Chelsea easily recognized her from the pictures in the newspaper of the charity auction.

"I'm sorry. I didn't mean to interrupt." God! Could this get any worse?

"It's no problem."

The woman looked at Vaughn.

Chelsea did, too.

He rebounded a lot better than she had. And why not? He obviously wasn't as invested as she was. She rubbed the sore spot in her chest where her heart had just taken a nasty tumble off the pile of hope she'd been stockpiling under it.

"Cha-Cha." Vaughn made hasty introductions. "This is Sydney Richards."

"Cha-Cha?" The woman cocked her head to one side. Offered her hand. Her eyes discreetly slid over Chelsea.

She wished she was something other than a carpenter. And for the first time in her life, she wished that *something* was someone... *feminine*.

She rubbed the sore spot in her chest again.

"That's an unusual name."

Sydney's voice was full of sophistication. No twang from the hills or the hollow, leaving Chelsea feeling lacking and lowly. And the woman was still looking at her. Really expecting some kind of response.

"Well, the boys… gave me that…" Again, the words eluded her. Chelsea didn't want to be here. She didn't want to talk about the stupid nicknames the boys used in the shop. The one Vaughn never used.

Except he had.

And why wouldn't he? He'd probably been so distracted by the gorgeous woman standing so near to him that Chelsea… well, she was—

"Chelsea," Vaughn quickly corrected himself. "This is Chelsea Chathford."

"Very nice to meet you, Chelsea."

And time moved forward with, or without Chelsea's participation.

The woman offered her hand, leaving her no choice but to shake it. And to compare how soft her palm was to her own rough one.

She rubbed the hurting spot in her chest again.

"You work for Garrett?" the woman asked.

"Vaughn," Chelsea and Vaughn both said at the same time.

"I'm sorry." Sidney smiled up at Vaughn. It was a beautiful smile. Warm and brimming with desire. And if Chelsea weren't filled with jealousy, she'd admire this woman's openness. Her unpretentiousness. It was obvious she had feelings for Vaughn. She placed a hand to her chest, inadvertently showing off beautifully manicured nails. "I must be the only person to call him that."

She was. And why was that?

"It's just Vaughn now," the man in question replied, leaving Chelsea to wonder why it was *just Vaughn now?* She couldn't imagine any reason why she would suddenly be *just Sophia Chathford now* instead of Chelsea Chathford. So why was he now Vaughn, and not Garrett?

Sydney was still looking at her.

Chelsea couldn't help but catalog their differences. Five-foot-ten plus to five-foot-six plus. A blond, no-fuss ponytail to golden brown tresses expensively cut, styled, highlighted, and whatever else the woman's beautician did to make her hair fall in perfect waves around her perfectly made-up face.

The cut was deep. Slicing right into the heart of her vulnerability.

"So... you work for Gar— Vaughn?"

"Yes. I do." Chelsea found the words for simple conversation. "I'm one of Vaughn's... employees," she added. More for herself than for Sydney Richards, who wasn't just beautiful; she was nice. Under other circumstances, Chelsea would like the woman. Not that they'd ever run in the same circles. Or ever be friends.

"Chelsea is my master carpenter," Vaughn added, further

reminding Chelsea of her place.

She rubbed her chest again. This was worse than anything she'd imagined. She should have gone home. At least then she'd still have her hopes. And her dreams.

All she had now was an ache in her chest where her heart had been bulldozed over.

"You're a carpenter?"

"Yes, ma'am." Chelsea winced at the part of Harlan County that had slipped out in her accent and ordinary politeness.

"That's remarkable, Chelsea. I'm very impressed."

Chelsea stuffed her hands into her front pockets. Stared at the floor. She didn't know how to respond. She wanted to hate the woman. She wanted to hate Vaughn. But she couldn't. And he... She chanced a glance. He looked as uncomfortable as she.

"Did you need something?" he pointedly asked.

A brain transplant came to mind. But before she could come up with a lie, one she wouldn't trip on later, he cupped his palm around her elbow. "We'll just be a minute," he told Sydney, as he towed Chelsea along beside him into his office.

He shut the door. Closing them off from the lobby. He dropped his chin to his chest. Heaved out a sigh. Slowly lifted his head. "It's not what you think. I swear it's not."

Guilt colored his words. Filled his eyes.

"It doesn't matter what I think." Not when there was a

gorgeous woman waiting for him on the other side of the door.

He stepped closer. "It *does* matter. *You* matter." His finger slowly brushed against her cheek. "She just stopped in. I didn't invite her here."

"Vaughn—" Could this get any more awkward? "You don't have to explain." And when she should step away from him, she couldn't move her feet.

"Yeah... I do." He leaned closer. His lips hovering near her temple. And she breathed in his musky scent. Her jaw nearly touching his. The heat of his body surrounded her. His mouth brushed against her temple. Hers touched his chin, rough with beard. His lips slowly slid down her cheek.

Willingly, she took what he gave.

Like scraps thrown out to the stray dog nobody wants. But can't get rid of.

"None of this, Chels." His mouth touched the corner of hers. And even as she allowed herself to kiss his chin, to slid her tongue along his jaw, and kiss his neck, she knew. She didn't want to be thrown scraps. She didn't want to be the stray.

She wanted to be the one. *The only one.*

"None of this is as it seems." And he looked so tortured. So torn.

And she found the strength she needed to face the truth. Painful as it was. She took one step away from him. Folded her arms across her chest. To contain the pain. "It looks like you have a date."

There. She shined a spotlight on the truth.

"Chels—"

He said her name with such weariness in his voice. He lifted his hand. To touch her.

"No." She put a hand out to stop him. "She's the one. Isn't she?" And she hated the wobble in her voice. The seething jealousy and hurt responsible for it. She had no claim on this man. Yet...

"She's the one from the auction, isn't she?"

And his lips pressed together. "I did your friend a favor!" He spit out the words in anger. "I didn't want to." His voice rose. His arm swung wide. "I didn't want to do any of it!"

"Vaughn." And Chelsea couldn't help but touch her palm to the center of his chest. "I know," she found herself saying, even though she didn't. Maybe he really liked the woman. Maybe he was just trying to find a nice way to let her down.

"It's that damn bachelor auction." His chest rose and fell with agitation.

"I know," she found herself saying again as holiday wishes and foolish hope refused to die inside her. "You're doing what's..." expected? Doing what was right? How did she know?

And deep-seated uncertainty found fertile ground to take root. Maybe he was secretly glad Sydney won him in the auction. Maybe he was doing what came natural — pursuing a beautiful woman who was obviously quite interested in him.

And there he was. Somehow reading her mind because his brow furrowed. His lips pressed together. And before she let her foolish heart crush her uncertainty, the corners of his mouth turned down. And maybe he wasn't reading her mind. Maybe he was just tired of her wasting his time. Keeping him from—

"Chels."

"No." Chelsea didn't want to listen. Didn't want to know. Her heart had been tripped up enough already. "Really. It's okay." She pulled her hand away from his chest. She curled her fingers into her palm to trap his warmth there for a little longer. And she stepped back. Away from him. Before she did something really stupid.

Like kiss him again.

Or ask him to go with her to the New Year's Eve Gala.

"I was just leaving." She folded her invitation in half. "I just wanted to say good night. And wish you a Merry Christmas." The next time she'd see him was, "Happy New Year, too, Vaughn." She took another step away from him. Her stupid eyes filling with tears. "I'll… I'll let you get back to your… guest."

He stopped her before she had a chance to slip the invite into her back pocket.

"You are still going to the party, aren't you?" His fingers slowly slid up and over hers. The calluses there igniting a fiery need inside her only he could quench.

But that wasn't going to happen. She wouldn't get what she wanted for Christmas. Or in the New Year either.

"Yes. I'm going." She refused to look at him beyond his chin. Refused to acknowledge the flames of awareness burning up her arm. Or the rush of desire that infused her from the inside out with hot yearning. And she refused to think about the beautiful woman patiently waiting for his affection and attention on the other side of the door.

He slowly nodded his head up and down. "That's good." He made no move to end this conversation. Or this erotic torture. "Maybe we could—"

"Chelsea?"

A man stood near the door of Vaughn's office and Vaughn's hackles rose.

"You ready?"

And before Vaughn could ask who the hell he was, or ask Chelsea out in spite of him – or Sydney – she spun out of his reach.

"Yes," she quickly replied. Heat flushed her cheeks.

Embarrassment? Guilt? Surprise?

They walked through the shop.

Vaughn followed them.

The man's hand rested possessively at the base of her spine with a familiarity Vaughn didn't like.

And he could do nothing but watch with frustration as the man held the back door open for her. Watch with jealousy as the man smiled down at her right before the back door shut, blocking his view.

Who the hell was this guy?

And before he could chase her out into the parking lot, demand answers—

"Garrett?"

Vaughn turned. Sydney was standing near. Her brows pulled together. How much had she witnessed?

"Are you okay?" She took a step closer. "You look angry."

"I'm fine." He relaxed his features. It was hard. He was pissed. Jealous. Angry at himself for letting opportunity get away. He should have asked Chelsea to go with him to the New Year's Eve Gala as soon as he'd gotten the invite.

The noose of responsibility tightened around his neck.

He couldn't be that reckless, that irresponsible again.

He had an obligation to Sydney. To Lauren. "Do you wanna go out tonight?" he impatiently asked.

"On our date?"

"Yeah." It was reckless. Crazy. It was thinking no further than his own personal gratification. It was Garrett Vaughn Jennings the Third as he'd been when he'd destroyed the Jennings legacy.

"It's kind of short notice, don't you think?"

"It's been a week since the auction." A week he'd wasted avoiding Chelsea, when all he really wanted to do was be with her. A week when he should have been squaring things away with Sydney. He ignored the voice in his head. The one that sounded like his father.

"We could go out tonight." They could. He could be charming. Polite. And in a few hours, his obligation to Lauren, and to Sydney, would be over. And he'd be free to—

She was shaking her head side to side. "I can't go out tonight. I already have plans."

"Change them."

"No. I can't." She frowned. "And I won't."

"Tomorrow then." The sooner he got this charity date out of the way, the sooner he could go after what he really wanted.

Chelsea.

"I'm sorry, Vaughn. I can't go out tomorrow either. Christmas time is full of family obligations. And social responsibilities."

"The next day."

She was already shaking her head.

"How about next week?" They could go out. Early in the week. And he'd still have a few days to ask Chelsea to the New Year's Eve Gala where it wouldn't look last minute. Or like she was his second choice, which she'd never been. And before his common sense could kick him in the ass for being an idiot, thinking like that, Sydney's brows lifted high over her eyes.

"Next week?" Her voice rose when she said *week*.

And he understood why. Christmas was next week. New Year's the following. But he had two weeks left in the year, and three holidays thrown into the mess. He was running out of time to fulfill his responsibility to Lauren – and his obligation to Sydney – before he could do something for himself.

"A little anxious aren't we, Garrett?" Coyly, she touched his arm, misreading his urgency. Her fingers lingered, drawing lazy circles on his wrist that did nothing for him. "I can't possibly squeeze in another activity next week. Not with Christmas."

"How about—"

She talked over him. "We make our date the New Year's Eve Gala at Bliss? What do you think?"

That he wanted to go to the Gala with Chelsea.

"It'll be fun, Garrett."

No employee dating.

He'd tried every damn trick, exhausted every idea to fulfill his obligations – his responsibilities – and still be able to ask Chelsea out. He wanted to take her to the Gala.

"What do you think?"

That no matter what he tried, the Forces of Nature were working against him. Keeping him on the straight and narrow. Despite his own wants and needs.

"You're not saying anything," Sydney hesitantly added.

"I'm sorry." He pushed down deep inside what he really wanted. It wasn't Sydney's fault. If he'd have followed through on his responsibilities immediately, like he should have, their date would be history. She'd be happy. Lauren would be happy. And Vaughn would have been free to ask Chelsea to the Gala as soon as they'd been given invites. Instead he was spewing lies, saying stupid shit like, "Yeah. That's... good."

And she was watching him, reading him better than if his responses had been plastered on a billboard. "It really is the only free night I have before the end of the year. But..." She worried her bottom lip with her front tooth. "If you have other plans..."

"No. That's fine," he lied. He even tried to punctuate it with a smile. It wasn't her fault. It was his. He'd been irresponsible. Again. *Just like old times, huh, dad?* "Really. It's... It's good."

"I'm glad." And she must have believed him. She stepped closer. Touched her palm to his chest. The same place Chelsea had just touched. And he worked really hard not to tense under her fingertips. Or to compare.

Any normal man would be ecstatic to have a woman like this sniffing around him. Instead he couldn't help but remember how pretty Chelsea looked standing in his office earlier that day, in her faded jeans. Her cheeks rosy red. Her eyes glowing. And how sad she looked standing in that same spot a few moments ago, tears filling her eyes.

He'd made her freakin' cry. He was the biggest ass on the planet.

Sydney's expensive perfume filled his nose. And he tried not to compare it to Chelsea's fresh scent. She always smelled so good. So natural.

"We can end this year together, Garrett."

He wished she wouldn't call him that.

"And then," her voice dipped with an intimacy he didn't feel. Would never feel. "We can start the new one together, too."

He should set her straight now. But it wasn't her fault he wanted another woman.

One he couldn't have. One he'd see at that damn Gala, with another man.

He was sure of it.

Chapter Eight

Lloyd was Chelsea's neighbor.

He'd picked her up at the shop after work. And he'd driven her to the garage so she could pick up her Jeep.

They were friends. With a failed relationship between them. And rather than lose who she was for the sake of a man's affection and attention, she'd said goodbye to the sex. And somehow they'd gotten over the breakup and had gone back to being just friends.

She should have told Vaughn that.

But she'd been so mad at him for being so closed-off. So twisted up inside and jealous, when she had no right to be, she'd left the shop with Lloyd by her side. And Vaughn's eyes boring holes right between her shoulder blades.

She wanted to stay mad at him. "But I can't," she mumbled under her breath. She dragged the Christmas tree she'd impulsively bought on the way home up three flights of stairs to her third-floor apartment.

"He'd done Lauren a favor being in that damn auction." She pushed open her apartment door. Deposited the tree in the center of her living room. He didn't want to do it. She knew that. But he'd done it anyway. She tossed her coat and gloves onto the couch. "And Sydney Richards looking all starry-eyed in his office was the result of that good deed."

She huffed out a breath of frustration. Dropped her head back in defeat.

He was a good man. A little over the top anal when it came to doing what he thought was right and responsible. He had one standard for the boys in the shop, and held himself to a higher, more rigid code. "Someday you will tell me why," she said, as she wrestled the Douglas fir into the tree stand in front of the window.

She stood back. She pulled the band from her hair. As she massaged the back of her scalp, she inhaled a deep breath. Savored the fresh smell of pine.

Nothing smelled like it.

Except the mountains of Kentucky.

"Maybe next year." She buried the sudden bout of homesickness. It would disappear when the holidays were over. When life returned to normal and she went back to her everyday routine of work.

When she should be admiring her holiday addition, thinking which ornaments she'd put out this year, her mind veered off course. And right into the mess that was her non-existent relationship with Vaughn. "What happened to make you so rigid? What happened to make you so tough on yourself?" So unrelenting. And—

"No more thinking about him. And wondering," she

firmly told herself. Not that it was even remotely possible. She was a Chathford. They were a stubborn lot. And Vaughn—

She rubbed her temples with her fingertips.

He was fulfilling an obligation. With another woman. And since it appeared she wanted to really be mean to herself. To stomp all over what was left of her wishes and dreams. At this very moment... "He might be starting a new relationship with the woman."

And why wouldn't he?

Sydney Richards was beautiful.

And he'd looked so guilty.

"You're not doin' this!" She exhaled a breath of frustration. She was not going to second-guess. Suppose, wonder, or even imagine. It might be the season of miracles, but, "There isn't one in your future," she sternly told herself.

She walked through her apartment. The owner of the building had done a terrible job breaking up the old house into rental units. But she'd been one of the luckier tenants. Although she hadn't gotten one of the bigger apartments on the first floor, or even the second floor, she had gotten one of two apartments on the top floor. The one with a turret. And once the landlord had known her profession, he'd given her carte blanche to renovate the space.

The first thing she'd done was turn the turret room into her bedroom. She'd opened up the ceiling, exposing wooden beams that radiated out from the center section like the rays of the sun. And she'd refinished all them.

There were a dozen tall, narrow windows that lined the rounded walls. And although she'd refinished the wood casements and covered them with drapes for the sake of her privacy, when opened, the position of the house on a rise gave her a spectacular view of Albemarle Sound.

Her papa had built her a sleigh bed. And he'd made her marble-topped nightstands. He was a furniture maker. Still holding out hope his only child would join him in the family business.

"Maybe sooner than you think, Papa," she said to herself, as she walked into the spare bedroom. The closet there was the catch-all for the clothes she rarely wore, which was most of her dress wardrobe and the Christmas decorations her papa had given her when her momma had passed on.

"I miss you, Momma," she softly said to the ethereal presence always with her. The one she could feel, especially now, as she pulled boxes and tools from the closet to get to her mother's decorations.

On top of one box, she found the newspaper with the photo spread of the celebrity auction. She picked it up. She didn't know why she'd kept it.

She knew exactly why.

But she wasn't sixteen anymore, and twenty-eight-year-old women didn't tape pictures of the men they had crushes on to their bedroom mirrors.

She stared at the picture of Vaughn looking all hot and intensely serious. And sexy. And then her eyes strayed to another picture. To the name below it. *Sydney Richards*.

"You're hard to compete with." Not that she was. He'd kissed her and ignored her. And Sydney Richards? She ran a finger down over the woman's picture. "You'll be going out with him." That's what she'd interrupted earlier in the lobby.

At least that's what she was telling herself she'd interrupted.

Chelsea sat down on the bed with the newspaper unfolded across her lap. She didn't know when she'd developed this sadistic streak. But it was with her, forcing her to look. And even more merciless, forcing her to compare.

Her eyes settled on the slender heels the woman wore in the picture. "I bet you don't own a pair of work boots." And why would she? She was a woman who didn't do manual labor. She wasn't a tradesman.

She was a lady.

Chelsea winced.

She was a lady. She could look feminine. She remembered how. It wasn't that long ago when she and her momma attended Sunday Socials at the Church of Christ in Cumberland.

She set the newspaper aside. Filled with renewed purpose, she walked over to her closet. She perused her meager collection of outfits. She pulled one dress off the hanger. Walked it back to her bed. Stripping down to her bra and panties, she slipped it over her head. And she twisted and contorted to reach the zipper. She sucked in a breath and held it. Sucked in her stomach. And still the zipper wouldn't budge beyond her bra clasp.

"Damn."

She'd put on a few pounds since she'd last worn it.

Thirteen years ago. To the last Sunday Social she and Momma had gone to. Right before her mother had died. "Definitely not a good choice." Too many memories. She chose to believe that, rather than the fact it was too tight. She tossed it to the floor.

More determined than before, she strode back to her closet. Moved a few hangers. It didn't take long to find another dress. There were only two more. She pulled the next selection off its hanger. Slipped it over her head. Breathed a sigh of relief when the long row of buttons from hem to bodice all buttoned. She ran an appreciative hand over the soft material.

She walked to the mirror. Winced at her reflection. "I look like Aunt Gert's drapes." And about as old. The large flowers and swirling colors were vintage. And dated. "Crap." She tugged on the buttons. Shimmied it over her hips and drop-kicked another bad choice from her past to the floor. It landed in a billowing heap on top the other dress.

She walked back over to the closet still holding out hope. She pulled the last selection from its hanger. It was black. "Classic," she said, as she slipped the dress over her head and shimmied it down over her hips. She grabbed the pair of heels she always wore with it and slipped them on. She adjusted the neckline as she walked over to the mirror. She looked at her reflection.

She turned her foot to the side. The two inch heels were nice.

Matronly a devilish voice whispered inside her head.

"Shut up." She stepped closer to the mirror. Studied her reflection.

It was pretty.

In a librarian sort of way, the devious voice whispered.

High neck. Sleeveless. *Plain.* "Classic," she told the irritating voice in her head. The one whispering, *boring.*

She turned to the side. Her eyes ricocheting from her dull reflection to the picture of Sydney Richards in her sparkling party dress with the tiny little straps. She dropped her head back. "I can't wear this!" Not to the Gala. What man wanted to stand beside a drape, or a nun? "No man," she told herself.

Especially not Vaughn.

"Forget him," she sternly warned herself, as she slipped the dress off her head. She tossed it to the growing heap on the floor. She added the stupid heels to the pile, too. Sat down on the edge of the bed. And tried really hard not to take center stage at her very own pity party.

"I don't have to go." She could stay at home. Sit right here, all by herself. Turn in early, and forget all about going to the gala.

But... Much as she'd never admit, even under guise of torture, she *wanted* to go. And she wanted to look like a knock-out when she walked into Bliss.

"It's stupid. You're acting stupid." She wiped her palms across her damp cheeks. Men didn't look at her like that. Ever. They respected her. They liked her. They considered her one of their own. But they didn't go scent-of-a-woman goofy over her.

She bent down, picked up the dresses that had been just fine going to Sunday Socials in the mountains of Kentucky. She rolled them up into a ball. Tomorrow she'd throw them in the trash. Not even Harrington's poor, or homeless, should be subjected to walking around in them.

She sat down on the bed. She cupped her elbows. Hunched over and tried not to stare at her reflection in the mirror. And she tried not to look at the pictures in the damn paper still lying open on the bed beside her.

And she tried really hard not to want to be something more than she was.

She rubbed the pain in the center of her chest.

Her entire life, she'd been okay being who she was. And two kisses from a man who was probably at this very moment, kissing another woman, and she was stuck, wanting to be something she wasn't.

Why couldn't she be happy being ordinary Chelsea Chathford?

She walked to the mirror. Scrutinized her reflection. She turned her head to one side. She had her mother's sapphire blue eyes and high cheekbones. Her papa's chin looked good on him, dominating and jutting out, but on her? She winced. "Nothing you can do about it." Her eyes slid up to her hair. She lifted the thick, golden strands. Allowed it to sift through her fingers. It wasn't professionally cut and styled for maximum poof, but it was long and blond. And she liked it that way.

So why couldn't she like herself the way she was?

She picked up her phone. Punched in the number for the only person on the planet who could come to her rescue. When Lauren answered, Chelsea wasted no time. "I wanna go to the New Year's Eve gala. And none of my clothes fit – unless I wanna be a nun. And I don't wanna be a nun. I wanna be—" She stopped. Her rant ran its course. Leaving nothing but the truth exposed. And it was heartbreakingly simple.

She wanted to be *sexy*. She wanted Vaughn to desire her. To want her.

And nothing Lauren could do would make that happen.

"I'm sorry." She rubbed the sore spot in the center of her chest. "I shouldn't be bothering you."

"Chels. You're my friend. You're not bothering me."

"I'm okay." Chelsea wiped a palm over her cheek. She'd wear the black dress. It wasn't like Vaughn was going to toss Sydney to the curb when he got a look at her. That was the stuff of fairytales. And holiday wishes. "I'm just gonna wear my black dress."

"I forbid it."

Chelsea frowned. "What?"

"You can't wear black."

"Why?"

"Because." Her friend was slow to add, "It's against the rules."

"You know what?" Frustration was slowly replacing the hurt. "I'm sick and tired of rules." And after today's go-round with Vaughn, she especially had no respect for ludicrous rules forbidding anything. "I'm wearing my black dress. Forget I called." She eyed the offending garment haphazardly thrown on the floor. Maybe she could rework the neckline. Or add a slit.

"No."

"What?" She scowled.

"I said, no. I have been after you forever to go shopping with me. And you always turn me down. Well, I'm not letting you do that this time. Merry Christmas, Chelsea. I didn't know what to get you. Now I do."

"We don't exchange gifts." Chelsea rubbed her forehead.

"We do now. And my gift to you is a shopping spree."

Chelsea dropped her head back.

"You can stop your groaning right now. We are going shopping. And you are going to love it."

"No. No, I won't." She hated shopping. "I changed my mind. I'm not—"

"Oh, no, no, no. We hit the stores tomorrow morning."

"I'm busy tomorrow." She wasn't. But she'd rather work side by side with Vaughn smelling of Sydney's perfume than navigate the crowds at the local mall. "It's almost Christmas. The mall will be packed."

"I am Lauren Foster-Forsythe. Do you actually think I'm taking you to the local mall?"

* * *

"Miss Chathford. So very nice to meet you."

Chelsea mumbled a reply. Tried not to look awkward. She stuffed her hands into the back pockets of her jeans. Just as quickly, she pulled them out. She rubbed them against her thighs. She had never shopped this way. This discreetly.

"Your shopping assistant will be with you in a moment."

This *personally*. "Th-thank you."

"Please, Chelsea." Lauren grabbed her hand and squeezed it. "Relax. Have some fun."

"I will— I am."

"You're not."

She pushed the hair she'd let down today from her face. "I'm just not used to having someone wait on me."

"It's all part of the Carmichael experience, Miss Chathford."

The sales associate had returned on silent feet. Startled, Chelsea mimicked Lauren, nodding her approval. No upbringing in Harlan County had prepared her for how to act here.

"Everyone who wins a shopping experience to our salon has that same reaction." The associate patted her hand before turning and leaving for a second time.

Chelsea tucked her head into her neck as hot color flooded her cheeks. "She thinks I won this." The woman could tell right off she didn't belong here. "Maybe I shouldn't..."

"Ignore her, Chels. You have as much right to be here as I do."

113

"I doubt that." Lauren was a country music sensation. Married to a NASCAR superstar. And Chelsea was the daughter of a furniture maker in Kentucky.

"You have as much right to own a beautiful dress as anyone else. And do not go all tomboy on me and tell me you're gonna wear some ancient dress you have in your closet. And don't look at me like that." She pointed a finger. "You might not realize this, what with you, rockin' blue jeans and work boots, but the nun look went out of style ages ago."

"I rock blue jeans?"

"Like nobody else."

It was balm to her badly bruised feminine vanity. A weak smile pushed up the corners of Chelsea's lips.

"It's true." Lauren inhaled a slow deep breath. "What I would give to have breasts."

"You do."

"And an hour-glass figure like you have."

"I don't have…"

"You do." Lauren squeezed her fingers. "Don't give up."

Chelsea dropped her gaze. She was done wishing for what might never be.

The associate returned.

"You can disrobe over there." She pointed to a screened-off side of the private dressing area. "And slip this on." She handed Chelsea a plush white robe. "Would you like a cup of coffee? Or a glass of wine while you wait?"

"No thank you, ma'am," Chelsea replied, taking the robe from the woman's hands.

"While you slip that on, I'm going to give Bobby Wayne a quick call. I'll be right back."

"Take your time," Chelsea replied, but deep down inside, she wished Lauren would stay right here. At least with her nearby, Chelsea didn't feel quite so out of place.

The exclusive shop was not normally open on Sundays. It wasn't open to the regular public during normal hours either. It catered exclusively to Harrington's elite. The rich and famous.

Like Lauren. Or Sydney.

Not Chelsea. And yet...

"Miss Chathford, I'll be your shopping assistant for the day. My name is—"

Chelsea turned. "Sarah?" Vaughn's former assistant. She gave the young woman a hug. "You work here now?"

Sarah returned Chelsea's embrace. "For the season, at least. Then..." She shrugged a shoulder.

"Has Josh found anything?"

Sarah shook her head side to side. "No. It's tough."

"You could always come back to Jennings." If Sarah wanted to come back, Chelsea would find a way to make Vaughn take her back. Josh, too.

"I loved my job there. But I love Josh more. And— "

Lauren walked into the room.

Sarah's eye went wide. "You're— You're—" A bad case of being star struck made her stutter.

"Lauren." Chelsea made the introductions. "Meet Vaughn's former assistant, Sarah Ashton."

Lauren smiled. "Nice to meet you, Sarah."

"You're— M-married to— Bobby Wayne Forsythe!" Sarah's hand splayed wide across her chest. "I can't believe I'm standing with *Lauren Foster-Forsythe!* Can I have your autograph?"

"Your friends with Chelsea?"

Sarah's head bobbed up and down.

"I'll do you one better." Lauren reached into her purse. She pulled out an ivory envelope. Scribbled her signature across the front of it. "You and—" Lauren lifted inquisitive eyes to Chelsea.

"Josh," Chelsea supplied.

"You— and Josh — are invited as my guests to the New Year's Eve Gala at Bliss."

"I can't believe I'm holding a personal invitation to the Gala at Bliss!" Sarah unleashed her excitement on Chelsea. "Are you going?"

"Yes."

"With Vaughn? He's crazy about you. I saw the way he looks at you."

Her friend was wrong. Chelsea had seen the guilt in his eyes. "I'm sure Vaughn will be going to the gala with…

someone else." And since it hurt too much to even think of him with someone else, even on a charity date, she asked, "Can we talk about something else? Like finding me a dress?"

* * *

Chelsea had been stripped down to her panties. Her body parts measured, her tastes cataloged. All that was left was to wait for Sarah to select dresses specifically tailored to meet her measurements and holiday needs.

"I don't suppose I could just wear—"

"No," Lauren replied.

"But you didn't even hear what I was going to say."

Lauren leaned closer. Rested her elbows on her knees. And she looked at Chelsea. "What's really wrong?"

Chelsea inhaled a slow, deep breath. "Am I so bad the way I am?"

Lauren's dark brows pinched together. "Are you serious?"

"Yes."

"Chels." Lauren reached over, laid her hand over Chelsea's. And Chelsea couldn't help but compare her short nails with their clear polish to her friend's manicured ones. "You are beautiful just the way you are." Her friend inhaled a deep breath. "I am so sorry. For messing up everything. I get so obsessed when it comes to Bliss."

Her friend did. There was no better guardian for the stately old mansion than the woman sitting beside her.

"I made Vaughn participate in the auction. He didn't want

117

to. He tried to get out of it."

"This isn't about Vaughn," Chelsea told her friend. "This is about me. All my life—" Struck suddenly shy, Chelsea stared at her hands in her lap.

"What, Chels?" Lauren softly prompted.

"All my life I've been the girl hangin' out with the guys. Never the girl getting chased and asked out by them."

"Then they were stupid."

"Apparently, that malady doesn't just affect sixteen and eighteen-year-olds."

Lauren lent a sympathetic smile. "There's nothing wrong with the way you look. And if you think I brought you here because there was, you're wrong. I brought you here to pamper you. You work hard. All the time. I want you to have a Cinderella moment and come to the ball. And I want your holiday wish to come true."

"You think I have one?"

"I know you do."

Her friend knew her well. "Can I show you something?"

Chelsea reached for her pants. Retrieved her wallet and handed Lauren an old photo.

"That's you?"

And she supposed the incredulousness in Lauren's voice was warranted.

"It was thirteen years ago. A church social back home. But Momma loved those things."

"I can't believe that's you."

"I have gone out on dates."

Lauren lifted her gaze. "I should hope so."

"I do know how to dress up."

"Like a nun," her friend teased.

"Which is why you dragged me here," Chelsea teased back before growing serious. "My momma died shortly after that picture was taken."

"I'm sorry, Chelsea."

"Papa didn't really know what to do with a teenage daughter." She gently ran a finger over the faded image of her mother. "He was hurting and so was I. And I guess," she laid the wallet in her lap. Folded her hands over it. "It was easier." She dipped her head. Picked at the corner of the leather. "To be a tomboy than a young woman who needed lots of fussin' over."

Chelsea lifted her head. Blinked her eyes. She was not going to cry over the choice she'd voluntarily made. There was no changing it. No fretting over it either.

"Except for a couple, all the pretty dresses got boxed. The makeup tossed out. The heels were buried deep in the back of the closet." Along with any teenage hopes Chelsea had of being a beautiful young woman who men chased after. Hopes she apparently still had.

"I'm not doing this to get Vaughn's attention," Chelsea told her friend before she tried to fix something that wasn't fixable. "I'm doing this for me. *I* want to remember what it's like to get dressed up. To *feel* feminine." And to have hope holiday wishes could come true.

Even if it was just for one night. And for no one but her.

* * *

Vaughn stood out in the parking lot, lifted his hand in a half-hearted wave, and watched as the taillights of Sydney's Mercedes disappeared around the bend in the road that led to Harrington. He turned. Wiped the back of his hand against his mouth as he headed to his shop. Once inside, he let out an exasperated breath.

He'd kissed her.

She'd expected it.

It was what he was supposed to do.

She'd done him a favor. She'd helped him out with the end-of-year books. She'd straightened out the mess that a herd of temporaries had left him when he'd foolishly fired the best office assistant he'd ever had. And she'd done it without him asking. And without demanding anything in return.

Except a kiss.

And he'd given her one.

After he'd crassly offered her money. For her services.

He offended her. He witnessed the hurt in her eyes. But she'd hidden it well. And what was he supposed to do after that kind of stupidity? He added another heaping helping on top of it. He gave her a damn kiss. He stomped his feet on the rug inside the lobby area. Turned and locked the door.

Guilt was riding him hard. Like he'd somehow been unfaithful to Chelsea. A woman he had yet to go out with. A woman he loved, yet never had.

"This?" He dropped his head back against the door. He let out a deep sigh. "This is my penance?" he asked the ghosts of his past. The guys in the shop had all left two days ago. Chelsea had been in an out, like she always was at the end of year. Except this year, she was avoiding him.

He didn't like it. Not one damn bit.

When he was in the office, she was in the shop. When he ventured into the shop, she high-tailed it out to the warehouse. If he followed, she found someplace else to disappear. All he'd wanted was to be near her. To talk to her.

And then Sydney had shown up. Unannounced. Unexpected. A godsend he had trouble being grateful for.

And Chelsea had left.

Giving him no chance to explain.

How did he explain an uninvited guest? How did he explain caving to another woman's wishes, or in Lauren Foster-Forsythe's case, demands?

He cussed. With the swipe of one hand, he cleared his desk of the stacks of folders and files Sydney had meticulously gone through and left there. "Is this what you wanted?" he yelled, as he threw open the door of his office. It banged against the wall. He marched into the shop. "Haven't I paid enough?" he yelled louder, pushing a half-finished chair out of his path. Its wheels screeched as they skidded across the concrete floor. "If I'da killed someone, I'd be out of jail free by now!'

His debt paid.

He swiped a hand across the work table. Boxes of screws and nails, cataloged and sorted earlier, spilled over the edge. He pushed at a pile of lumber. The boards toppled, clattering against the concrete floor. He pounded a fist against a metal cabinet. "I made a mistake, *dammit!* A mistake." His hands curled into fists. He pressed his forehead against them. His chest heaved from exertion. And the words he'd never admitted to, spilled out of him. "I was young. I was stupid. I thought she loved me.

"Stupid." He heaved out a sigh of regret. He leaned his back against the cool metal. "Yeah, I know," he said a little quieter. A little saner. "I never meant for any of the shit that followed to happen. I'm sorry. Okay?" He sucked in a sharp breath. It punctured the tortured memories roiling around inside him. "So damn sorry."

He bent over. Re-stacked the mess he'd made of the boards. He rested a hand on the top of the pile. Bowed his head. "I can't change the past. And I don't wanna do penance for it the rest of my life." He looked over at Chelsea's workstation. "I love her."

He bent down. Picked up the boxes of nails and screws he'd angrily knocked to the floor. He carefully re-sorted them. "I don't know when it happened, Dad, but it did. And I know what you'd say... if you were here. And I..." He exhaled another breath of regret. "You don't know how many times I wish you were."

He dropped his head to his chest as the memories rose up, with less power this time. "I loved the sex Linda gave me. I thought she loved me. But you were right. She was using me." Giving him everything he wanted and some things he'd only fantasized about. And while he'd been blinded by lust, she'd been sabotaging his family's business. "It's different this time, Dad. I love Chelsea." And he was old enough – and maybe wise enough – to know the difference.

He paused. His hand resting on the half-finished chair he'd dragged back into place. And he didn't know if he was waiting for his father's scoff. Or his forgiveness. "I made a mess of my life. Of our lives. I'm sorry. You'll never know how very sorry I am. But I'm building something new here. And Chelsea. She's been a part of it from the beginning. As much a part of it, as I am. I don't wanna be alone, Dad. Not like you." Not like the man who'd lived his entire life without a woman in it. At least not after the one who, when his parents had divorced, had taken a cash settlement in exchange for her son. He'd never seen his mother after that.

"I can't live like this anymore." Not like he'd been doing for the last five years. "I want Chelsea. And you know what? I'm sorry. I'm not you. I don't have that kind of will to stand on your rules and principles. I want Chelsea in my life. And I'm gonna have her."

Tonight, if possible.

It was well past the dinner hour by the time Vaughn had cleaned up the mess he'd made of his office and his shop. The streets of Harrington were filled with last-minute shoppers. Men and women dressed in period clothing stood outside the

Mount Bethlehem Baptist Church singing Christmas carols in four-part harmony. There was a Santa Claus on every corner. Garland with red bows decorated the street lamps that lined the main street of town. Snow spit down from the nighttime sky, the crystals glistening in the truck's headlights.

Leaving the yuletide chaos on the main street, he followed a maze of turns and side streets, pulling the truck into an empty parking spot outside the Victorian Chelsea lived in. In the silent, heavy air the truck's engine ticked as it cooled.

Her apartment was easy to spot. Aside from the fact he knew she lived on the third floor, she was sitting on a stool in the window. A naturally beautiful Madonna surrounded by the twinkling lights of the Christmas tree behind her. A sparkling backdrop to her beauty. And she was beautiful.

He'd always thought so.

Outside. And inside, where it really mattered.

She held an ornament in her hand. Much like she did with a piece of wood when she was crafting a replica, or renovating an antiquated one, her long graceful fingers slid over what she was holding. Her attention, hell, her spirit was reaching out, connecting with the past.

She had a way of doing that. Reaching into the past.

What would she do with his? If she had a chance to know it?

The light from the chandelier shined down on her golden head. Her long blond hair fell down over her shoulders. His heart filled with joy, his soul with peace and happiness every time he looked at her. Every time he thought of her.

He opened the door. Stepped down. He pocketed the keys. And before he could second-guess his decision, he clicked the lock on the door and shut it. He turned to cross the street at the same time a dark-colored van pulled into the Victorian's driveway.

Vaughn paused two steps into the slushy street.

The man who'd picked up Chelsea at the shop stepped out of the van, pocketing his keys as he walked up the steps to the old house. Without pause, he opened the door.

Like he had every right to.

Chelsea stood. She stepped away from the window. Was she expecting this man?

Of course, she was. He'd picked her up at work. And now he was walking into her apartment building. Helpless fury engulfed Vaughn. And jealousy. The man had a key to open the front door. Did he have a key to open her apartment, too?

And before Vaughn could witness gut-wrenching confirmation, he turned. Unlocked the truck and climbed back in. He stabbed the key into the ignition and pulled away. No closer to having what he wanted than five years ago, when she'd walked into his shop, a beautiful answer to his prayer.

Chapter Nine

Lauren's gracious holiday gift had been the salve needed to soothe Chelsea's battered spirit. Spending the day with her, and Sarah, trying on clothes, picking out a few new things for every day, had been something Chelsea hadn't done since her momma had died. She hadn't realized how much she'd missed being a woman instead of one of the guys in the shop.

Deep down inside she'd always prefer jeans to a dress. She'd always find the most pleasure working with her hands instead of having someone working on hers. It's who she was. And before she worried that little insight into something more than the natural order of things, she gathered up the fix-ins for a holiday meal, tossed a few of her newly purchased items into an overnight bag, and drove home to Harlan County.

She spent the Christmas holiday with her papa. If he noticed her distress, he didn't say. They'd gone to church on Christmas Eve. Sat in the same pew she'd sat in a thousand times with her momma. There was comfort in that. Blending the old with the new. They sang the hymns heralding the arrival of the Christ child. Lifted their candles to a silent, holy night, and filled the church to the rafters afterward with joy to the world because the Savior had come.

And then they'd gone home. Sipping glasses of Jim Beam, they sat in comfy overstuffed chairs by a warm fire blazing in the fieldstone fireplace. Together they quietly awaited the arrival of Christmas while big, fat flakes of snow gently fell from a midnight blue sky blanketing the land all around them.

As they always did, early in the morning, they exchanged gifts tucked under a live Christmas tree. After the holiday, when the cold winter yielded to the warmer days of spring, her father would plant it in the yard out by the shop.

Spring would come. A new year, too. And while a turkey cooked in the oven and her papa tinkered in his shop, Chelsea walked the trail that led to the mountains surrounding her childhood home. It helped her sort through her emotions. And her dilemma with Vaughn.

Two days later, she drove home. She stayed away from the shop. It was hard. It had been her routine for the last five years. And time she treasured. Just Vaughn. And her. Working together, Clearing away one year. Planning and anticipating another.

She wasn't sure yet what she was going to do. She couldn't take another year living in limbo. Loving someone who didn't feel the same way she did. Could she pick up and start over? And if she did, where?

She exhaled a sigh of uncertainty. Her life was a mess.

Yet time went on. It was New Year's Eve. Her night to set aside all her problems and enjoy herself. Maybe even, as Lauren had suggested, have a little fun.

Any life-altering moments would have to wait until the

arrival of the New Year.

She turned onto the shell driveway leading to Bliss. Taking her place in a long line of luxury automobiles and sports cars, she slowly inched the Jeep forward. A stable of young men with wool scarves wrapped around their necks and gloves on their hands scurried around. Some opened doors, helping formally-dressed ladies from their cars while others slid behind the wheel pulling the car away.

She wiggled in her seat. Nerves, most likely. She wasn't wearing a bra. The dress she'd chosen for herself didn't allow for one. Her panties were silk. The cut something she never imagined she'd buy, much less wear. And they took getting used to. Her four-inch heels were high.

She pulled down the visor. Flipped open the lighted mirror and checked her reflection one more time. She rubbed a tiny fleck of lipstick from her front tooth. Turned her head side to side. She'd pulled her hair up on top her head. Allowed a few loose strands to frame her face.

Her mother used to do that with her own blond hair.

"What do you think, Momma?" she quietly asked the soft presence always near. She touched the silver earrings she wore. They had been her momma's.

You clean up real good, child.

Her momma's voice was as clear in her head as it had been thirteen years ago. She pulled up into the circular driveway in front of the mansion.

A valet held her door open. "Welcome to Bliss."

129

"Thank you." She took his offered hand, stepping down. Tried not to be thrilled his eyes never left her legs, but she was. And while the Jeep disappeared around the back of the house, she turned. Looked up at the stately brick mansion built before the Civil War.

White lights illuminated the trees and bushes surrounding the big old house. Golden light spilled from the mullioned windows on the first floor, washing over the holly and pine garland covering the stone window sills. Pine wreaths with festive red bows, cinnamon sticks and berries decorated the front doors. As it had a century ago, the golden flame of a single candle lit every darkened window on the second and third floor.

A roll call of names slipped through her mind. Olivia Harrington and Adam Calendar. Jane Harrington and Brennan Brown. Mary Elizabeth Callahan and Colin Harrington. April Harrington and Hale Abercrombie. Bobby Wayne Forsythe and Lauren Foster-Forsythe. Generations of love had been found within the walls of this grand old house.

She'd found love in here, too. Only difference? Hers was one-sided.

The front doors opened. Bobby Wayne and Lauren, the latest guardians of Bliss stood in the entryway. With Bobby Wayne's hand resting on Lauren's shoulder, they shared an intimate look before he dipped his head and kissed his wife.

Chelsea wanted that kind of devotion. That kind of love.

And before she could talk herself out of leaving, Bobby Wayne turned back into the crowd. Lauren stepped out onto the entryway. "Chelsea!" her friend called out and she had no choice, like time itself, but to move forward.

At the entryway, Lauren grabbed her hand. "I wasn't sure you'd show up," she said, wrapping her in an exuberant hug.

Chelsea hugged her back. "I told you I was coming." *And you're staying*, her conscience told her before she made up a lame excuse to escape. This was her night. Her date with destiny.

Lauren's eyes did a slow once-over. "You look… stunning. I knew that dress would be gorgeous on you. Come on." Lauren slipped her arm through Chelsea's. "I want to introduce you to some people."

Chelsea looked down at her friend, adopting the same determined glare she used on any of the boys in the shop. And she added a pointed finger as additional warning. "Not Luke Branson."

Her friend raised her hands. Palms up. "Absolutely not," she agreed. A little too easily. "He'll seek you out all by himself."

"No Trey Daniels either." Chelsea felt the need to set some rules of her own. "Or Derek Holmes. No Nashville starlings. No NASCAR superstars. Just Harrington folk."

Like Vaughn.

Chelsea pressed a palm over the pinch in her heart. She thought she'd had all the wayward thoughts of him corralled. Buried down deep. One hadn't slipped out to trip her up for at least an hour.

Lauren turned. Seriousness settled over her features. "He's here."

Chelsea nodded her head. "I knew he would be," she quietly replied, facing what she'd been trying to avoid for a week.

Lauren squeezed Chelsea's forearm. Her earlier levity replaced with pained solemnness. "I am so sorry, Chels. For how I ruined things. I had no idea. I would never have asked him to be part of that bachelor auction, if I had known."

"It's not your fault." This whole mess was no one's fault.

"I feel so responsible."

"You shouldn't."

"He didn't want to do it. From the beginning. But you know how I am. I kept pushing him to call her. I wanted everything from that night squared away by year's end. I didn't know. You and— he—" Lauren let out a slow exhale of breath. "I hurt you. I never meant to do that. And I feel so bad." Her friend's voice wavered. "So—"

"Will you stop?" Chelsea pleaded, hoping to avoid tears. She'd cried enough already. "I understand. I do." She didn't have to like it. For certain, she didn't. And she'd decide how to proceed with the rest of her life... later. "For now," she added. "Can I just have a little fun?"

With introductions out of the way and Lauren quickly moved onto another group of guests, Chelsea held the crystal tumbler of Jim Beam in her hand. A couple men approached her, interested; but she wasn't, and their polite conversation quickly waned and they moved on.

She found a quiet corner in the back of the grand foyer where she could soak up the festive atmosphere in contemplative solitude as she waited for the clock to strike twelve.

Lauren and the Historical Society had outdone themselves. The home was beautifully decorated. A cascade of bright red poinsettias in gold foil-wrapped pots filled one side of the marble staircase. White lights entwined in green pine garland hung from the mahogany bannister, held in place with large, red velvet bows. She smiled to herself remembering when it had been painted to look like an asphalt NASCAR track. Huge evergreens stood in festive sentinel in the entryway, their branches adorned with twinkling white lights and gold ornaments. Pine and vanilla scented the air.

In one corner, a twelve-piece ensemble played soft music. Couples dressed in formal attire danced under the glittering crystal chandelier. She caught a glimpse of Sarah and Josh.

And then Vaughn.

With Sydney.

They made a striking couple what with Vaughn's dark hair and bright blue eyes. That he was taller than most of the men in the room only served to accent Sydney's delicateness. They stood close together. Like a couple. Sydney did a lot of leaning in and smiling up at Vaughn. And Vaughn, although he didn't smile, did appear to be attentive.

Chelsea looked away. Tonight was about moving forward. Without him. She rubbed the stinging spot in her chest the thought left behind. Hoping to avoid another awkward encounter like the one in the shop, she strolled around the edges of the party. She slipped down a few of the halls veering off the grand foyer. Peeked into the many rooms she'd helped Vaughn restore.

Ruthlessly, she pushed his memories aside, concentrating on what was in front of her. What she'd helped to change.

Each room was decorated differently to reflect one of the previous owners. It was Lauren's way of connecting and blending the present with the past. In Bobby Wayne's study, Olivia Harrington's antique desk – the one Chelsea had restored – still sat there in stately elegance. Her antique pistol was encased in glass on one wall along with framed photos of Bobby Wayne's win at the Daytona 500 and the infamous picture taken of the NASCAR great and Lauren at his last race. A twelve-foot evergreen stood in one corner decorated with memorabilia from Forsythe Racing.

Chelsea moved on. Her palm rested on the mahogany door frame leading into the dining area decorated purely British. The long table was elegantly set for high tea, to honor Lady Jane Harrington. A laden table reflecting Brennan Brown's Irish heritage stood near the large windows in the rear of the room. The ones looking out into the beautiful garden the Irish gardener had crafted for the lovely widow while he mended and won her heart.

"Such history," she whispered.

"Such beauty."

Chelsea quickly turned.

A handsome stranger leaned against the door frame, making himself at home in her solitude. His eyes hovered over her breasts. "I'm sorry. But I was enthralled by your beauty—"

He wasn't interested in her. Not really. He liked what he saw. The dress, the heels, and upswept hair – she was the package under the Christmas tree – the one with the pretty paper and glittery ribbon. Everyone wanted to open that one.

And this man was no different.

But if he saw her on the street, in her jeans and tee shirt, he wouldn't take notice. His feigned interest had an ulterior motive. He wanted to get laid. And much as Chelsea tried to feel flattered, she felt hollow. And the earlier anticipation of this evening lost some of its glow. "That's the best you've got?"

He laughed.

He had a nice laugh. A nice smile, too. Her cynicism retreated.

"Okay, so you're the hottest chick at this party." He took a sip of his bourbon. "And I wanna get to know you."

"Liar." Yet Chelsea found herself relaxing in his company. "Does any truth come out of your mouth?"

"Not unless it absolutely has to." He took another sip of his bourbon. Finishing it in two swallows.

He was drinking. A lot. But it wasn't her problem. She was here for carefree fun tonight.

"So let me guess." He held up one finger. His eye narrowed as he stared at her face a few seconds before his gaze slid down over her body, lingering here and there. "You're… an underwear model."

"Uh…" she mimicked his pause. "No."

A pretty young waitress wearing a bright white tuxedo shirt and black satin bowtie appeared at his side with another glass of bourbon. He leaned into the young woman. "Thank you, darlin'." His lips brushed against her temple. He discretely slipped her a few dollars and she left with a rosy blush on her cheeks.

So he was a player. She was, too. Until it was time to retire her Cinderella persona and escape to her room. Alone. Taking another sip of her Jim Beam, she moved on. He walked beside her. His fingers teased the base of her spine exposed by the deep vee of her dress.

There was no tingle. Nothing like when Vaughn touched her, or—

She cut off those thoughts before they ruined her evening. She had an admirer. It was nice. End of subject.

She picked up their conversation thread. "I'm not an underwear model." In fact, she'd be glad when she could slip into her regular briefs. Tomorrow. When she returned to being plain, ordinary Chelsea Chathford. But for tonight, she played into the full Cinderella fantasy, complete with wishes, hopes, and dreams. Maybe even a charming prince.

She lifted her hand to her admirer. "I'm—"

He took her hand in his. "Don't tell me." His lips brushed against her knuckles. "Let me guess." His brown eyes twinkled, and she tried not to compare him to Vaughn.

This man liked her. Would he like her when she told him she was a carpenter? Would he still think her the hottest chick at the party? Or a mannish feminine hybrid?

"You…" He tapped his finger against her bottom lip. "You are a member of the Swedish Volleyball team."

She laughed, dislodging his finger. "Do I look like a volleyball player?"

His eyes settled on her face. His finger that had been tapping her bottom lip slowly slid down her neck, making teasing circles at the base of her throat… and lower. And still no spark of attraction. "You look like a beautiful woman." His voice dropped to a seductive hush as he leaned into her.

Definitely a man on the make.

She wasn't ready yet to pull away. She tapped her glass against his instead. "You drink a lot?"

"Maybe. Probably." He lifted his glass to his lips. "But not enough for my eyes to deceive me." He leaned an arm against the wall. Fingered a lock of her hair. He dipped his head close. "You are beautiful. And I'd like to get to know you better." He took another healthy swallow of bourbon.

The pretty young waitress from before magically appeared by his side. She offered him another full glass. He either paid well. Or the waitress was definitely smitten. The young woman disappeared into the woodwork.

Chelsea crossed her arms. "Okay, so who are you?"

"Eager?"

"Curious."

"I work for Team Forsythe. I grovel at Bobby Wayne's feet. Bow down to his every dictate."

There was a definite bite to his words. Jealousy? Envy? Or

something else?

"Isn't that the only way a body gets an invite here?"

"No," she told him. "You could be from Harrington. You could work in Nashville."

Or you could be a carpenter who didn't belong here anymore than the black asphalt paint with the yellow stripe had belonged on the Italian marble steps in the foyer.

Wake-up call!

She didn't belong here. Playing dress-up. Going through the motions. Pretending to be interested in this man. It wasn't going to make her forget Vaughn.

Cinderella's ball was over. It was time to go home.

"It was very nice talking to you. But I'm going to—"

"Wait." His fingers touched her shoulder. And for the first time since he'd walked up to her, he was really looking at her. "You aren't from around here, are you?"

Was it that obvious? Even to a stranger?

"You have an accent, darlin'. One you probably don't realize slips out when you talk."

Great. Just great.

"I have the same one."

He didn't.

"I'm Lucas Hart. Originally from Cowcreek, Kentucky." His words were coated with the mountain dialect of home.

"That's probably the first honest thing you've said to me

all night."

"Probably." He took another sip from his bourbon. "Can we start over?" He offered his hand.

She took it. "I'm Chelsea Chathford. Originally from Harlan County."

"Nice to meet you, Chelsea." He raised her hand to his mouth. His lips were cool, wet from the bourbon. He pressed a kiss to her knuckles. "What do you do, Miss Chelsea Chathford?"

"I'm an underwear model. For the Swedish Volleyball team."

He laughed. Clinked his glass against hers. "I deserved that."

"Yes, you did." She lifted her glass to her lips. Took a swallow and couldn't help but be reminded of the last time she and Vaughn had shared a drink. She missed him.

"Would you like another?" Lucas asked.

"No, thank you." She was still nursing her first one. She'd lost track of how many he'd had. Yet, he didn't look drunk. Didn't slur his words. Or stumble.

"So," he took another sip. "What do you really do, Miss Chelsea?"

"I'm a carpenter."

"A carpenter, huh?" He scowled. Shrugged a shoulder. "Doesn't matter. I still think you're beautiful." And he went into his spiel. The one he thought would get him laid.

It shouldn't matter, but it did. Vaughn only saw her as an employee. This man only saw her as an easy lay.

No one saw her for what she really was.

He leaned into her. Smiled as he played with a lock of her hair that had escaped from the pile atop her head. Too bad she knew he was only interested in her because of how she looked tonight. *Hot... sexy... feminine.* She exhaled a breath. She'd accomplished her goal. She'd gotten a man to notice her. She'd gotten what she wanted.

Damn shame it didn't make her anywhere near happy.

Sydney had social status. Family connections. And she was graciously offering them up to Vaughn with every introduction she made. And with every introduction, Vaughn felt more and more like an ass. A user. A player.

And he hated it.

"I can't do this." He turned. Spotted the woman he wanted to be with. Laughing. Smiling. Walking around, enjoying the attention of the man who hadn't left her side since she'd gotten here. Vaughn knew. He'd been watching her.

"Vaughn." Sydney stepped in front of him. "What are we doing?" Weariness and hurt filled her voice.

He pulled his eyes away from Chelsea.

"It's her, isn't it?" she quietly asked, and he could no longer lie. "It's always been her," she added, and he wondered how she knew. How she could read him so well, when he'd been trying so hard to hide it.

"I don't know what you're talking about," he testily replied, knowing he was still hiding. Still lying. Still playing a game he didn't want to play.

Her eyes narrowed. Her mouth pressed down on the corners. "Respect me enough not to lie to me. It's Chelsea, isn't it?"

"What do you want me to say?" It had been Chelsea for the last year. Little by little, over the last five years, he'd fallen in love with her.

"A hundred other things than that."

"I'm here. With you. Okay?" He'd do what he was supposed to do. And, coupled with the destruction he'd made of his chances with Chelsea, maybe it would balance the scales and somehow make up for the destruction he'd caused his father, and his grandfather.

"No. You're not really here with me."

"Yeah. I am." She was pissing him off. "This is our date," he reminded her. He was doing what he was supposed to do. What was expected. And he was counting the hours, the minutes, the freakin' seconds, until it was over and he could just get out of here. Away from the people who were having fun. Away from the happy crush of humanity ringing in the New Year with the person they loved.

"You're not on a date. You're *fulfilling* an obligation."

"What do you want from me?" He unleased the aggravation, the frustration, and the anger building inside him since he'd agreed to be part of that stupid bachelor auction.

141

"Obviously." Pain filled her eyes. "More than you can give me."

His lips pressed together. "I'm sorry, okay?" He hated hurting her. "I never promised anything more." She was a nice woman. Just not the woman for him. "Look—"

"Just forget it, Garrett."

"Don't call me that!"

She looked away. Dipped her head.

"Sydney." He didn't know why he was even trying.

She took a step away from him. Lifted her head. "I'm releasing you of your obligation."

"I made a promise." To Lauren. And to her. "I'm keeping it."

"No." She put her hand up, palm out. "I'm an analyst. I read and interpret market trends. And you." She touched her fingers to his jaw. "Much as I wanted, you were never on the market."

"Look. I never promised more than a date. I never—"

"I know." Blessedly, she interrupted him before he could make things worse. "I had just... hoped... for more."

"I'm sorry." He didn't know what else to say. He'd used this woman since he'd met her. Intentionally, and unintentionally. It appeared he was only a better person when he was with Chelsea.

She held out her hand. "Thank you. For the... date."

And he shook her hand, feeling like the biggest ass. "I'll drive you home." It was the least he could do. Tomorrow he'd write a check to Lauren to cover what this woman had paid for him at the auction. And then he'd write another one for the aggravation he'd caused both of them.

"No." She pulled back her hand. "I'm not ready to leave."

He was happy she was relieving him of his duty. He was mad he'd screwed up something so simple as a charity date. Pissed he'd hurt her, probably disappointing Lauren, and blowing any chance he had to be with Chelsea.

He couldn't seem to do anything right anymore.

"I hope, Vaughn." She stood on the tip of her toes. Brushed a chaste kiss against his cheek. "I hope the New Year brings you everything you desire." She turned, disappearing into the crowd.

"Sydney. *Sydney*," he called out again, as he stepped around a group raising their glasses in a toast. He didn't know why he was chasing after her. She gave him a graceful way out. Why couldn't he just accept it and move on?

Because you never could do what was right. Never could do what was expected of you.

And the voice in his head made him pause. And cuss. And realize for the first time since the mess in Savannah. "I'm done, Dad." He was done trying to get forgiveness from a dead man. And he was done here. He tugged on his tie. Turned in the direction of the unfinished wing of the house. The party was over for him.

He bumped into, "Sarah. Josh." The couple he'd fired. "How are you?" It was lame. But it seemed lame was the best he could do nowadays.

"How do you think?" Josh growled.

Sarah touched his hand, stifling him. "We're okay." They weren't. Strain pulled at the corners of her eyes. It hadn't been there when they'd had jobs with him.

Now was the time to correct another mistake he'd made.

"What I did, firing you—" He inhaled a deep breath. "I was wrong. I made a mistake and I'm very sorry." It was hard to admit. No wonder he'd screwed up so badly in Savannah. But he went on, needing to do something right tonight. "I should not have fired you."

"Damn right, you shouldn't have."

"If you are willing to forgive me." He looked at Sarah, the more reasonable and understanding one. "I want to offer your old job back to you. With a raise. And a promotion to office manager. And, Josh," he turned his head to the hard sell. "I'd like to offer you back your old job, as well. With a raise."

"I'm not giving up Sarah."

"I'm not asking you to. As far as I'm concerned, the shop rule has run its course." *It's over, Dad. I'm done.* "The rule is officially retired, and rescinded. You're free to work at Jennings and date whoever you want."

Josh pulled Sarah close to his side. "It's obvious who I want." The couple shared an intimate smile before, at Sarah's silent urging, Josh offered Vaughn his hand. "Thank you. I—"

"*We* accept your job offers," Sarah said with a smile on her face.

"Thank you," Vaughn replied. "Happy New Year."

All he wanted was to escape to his room. He felt drained. Like he'd climbed a thousand mile trek, straight up a mountain. He weaved through the burgeoning crowd as the revelers gathered, eagerly awaiting the countdown of the old year. In Vaughn's opinion, it couldn't come soon enough.

"Excuse me," he said for the about the fiftieth time as he finally escaped the crowd. "I won't be needing these," he told a waiter, handing back a couple noisemakers and a stupid-looking hat. He pulled the knot of his tie further down his chest. He unbuttoned the top two buttons of his shirt. Ran his hands through his hair, rubbing the pain in his head.

Leaving the chanting and laughter behind, he wearily made his way through the kitchen area, down a series of turns and up the stairs to the unfinished wing. His feet dragged across the faded Aubusson rug that still ran down this hallway. Old fashioned light sconces on the wall were turned down low, like a dimly lit beacon to his destiny.

He paused. Leaned against the wall. Dropped his head back. Closed his eyes and pressed his palms into the sockets. He breathed his first breath of freedom in five long years.

He was done.

No more living to please a dead man. In trying, he'd messed up his life worse than he'd messed it up in Savannah. "From this point, I live my life the way I want."

Of course, he'd live it without Chelsea.

145

She was lost to him. He'd seen her disappear down the hall with that man. She was probably at this moment—

"Vaughn?"

He opened his eyes. Couldn't believe what he was seeing. *"Chels."*

She was standing in front of him, a glittering vision of goodness. And perfection. His heart beat faster. His blood pushed harder through his veins. Burning hunger gnawed at his groin. She was looking at him with those beautiful blue eyes. And they were filled with concern. And worry. And—

"Are you okay?" she quietly asked.

"Do I look okay?" He growled. Like a wounded animal. Because everything he wanted was so close, yet unattainable because of his stupidity. "I'm not okay, all right? I miss you. I want—" And he caught himself before he begged. Exhaled a breath of pent-up frustration. "I just want this evening to be over. I want this freakin' year to be over. I want—"

"Shhh." She touched her finger to his lips. She stepped closer. Her legs slipped right between his. Her breasts a deep breath away from brushing against his chest, and the gnawing need to have, to possess, bit harder into his groin. Her scent, her sweet, sexy scent – an uncomplicated mix of body wash and shampoo – enveloped him. Like her calm steady presence.

She looked up.

And he could look at her for the rest of his life. Find no one more beautiful. More perfect.

She pressed her palms to his cheeks.

Want and need flooded his groin. His erection surged up, pushing hard into the zipper of his fly. And he was too weary, too beaten down to do anything but—

"I know what you want," she told him. Her breath was warm against his face. Sweet. Like she was. "I have exactly what you need," she softly added, right before she melted over him and pressed her lips to his.

Chapter Ten

Chelsea had never seen him look so tortured. So weary. Had never felt his hold so tight. Or so desperate. Like somehow he'd lose her. He needn't worry. He'd had her respect and her trust for five years. Her heart for the last three-hundred-and-sixty-five days. And her undying love for the rest of his life.

She wouldn't ask – or guess – where his date was. Or why he'd been waiting, listing like a battle-weary soldier against her bedroom door. She'd take instead, everything Fate was offering. Everything he was willing to give. And somehow with her tongue deep in his mouth she was able to insert the old key into the lock.

The door swung wide. Bounced off the inside wall. And the two of them, still locked in each other's arms, tumbled into the room. She caught the door on the rebound. Kicked it shut with her heel. She broke the kiss. Long enough to take in a much-needed breath. Her senses filled with his scent. Her nerves tingled with anticipation.

"I have wanted you for so long." He slowly slid his knuckles along her jaw. His voice was hoarse. "You are so beautiful." His fingers slowly slid down her neck.

Her breasts grew heavy with anticipation.

"The whole freakin' night, I could look at no one else but you." His big hand spread wide, teasing the top of her chest.

The tantalizing gesture did amazing things to the wet, throbbing spot between her legs.

His index finger slowly slid along her shoulder, pushing a tidal wave of need into her chest. It slipped under the strap of her dress. "You look hotter than hell in this." He leaned into her. His other hand slipped under the hem. "So hot." His palm slowly edged up her thigh.

"Vaughn." She breathed out his name. Her head dropped back in pleasure. His hot breath teased her neck. It was erotic torture. The best kind. His lips a mere exhale away from touching her skin, setting her on fire.

She grabbed the tie he had haphazardly unknotted halfway down his chest. Held tight. He was her anchor. Her bliss. Her holiday wish come true.

She brushed her breasts, still covered in satin and sequins, against his chest.

He growled his approval. His mouth touched, scorching her skin on contact.

She hissed her pleasure.

His tongue laved the spot, setting it on fire. His other hand slowly and methodically made its way further up her thigh to tease the edges of the silk panties she wore.

She slipped an ankle around his leg, inching her heel up the back of his calf. And up higher until she could wrap it around his waist.

"You drive me crazy." He wrapped his hand around her ankle. Teased the sensitized skin with his thumb. Erotic wild circles. Unparalleled excitement built inside her.

"You're doing a pretty good job yourself," she gasped, as he slipped one finger, then two into her briefs.

"You inspire me."

"Good to know," she breathed out as she opened her mouth. She brushed her lips against his neck. Tongued his skin, rough with stubble.

There was no sound more exciting, more empowering than the growl of pleasure escaping his lips.

"More." He slipped his fingers free of her panties. "I gotta have more." He cupped her backside with his palms and easily lifted her off her feet. For that alone she would love him. He made her feel feminine. Sexy.

She wrapped both legs around his waist. Slid her fingers into his hair. Their mouths melded together. He carried her to the bed. Carefully laid her down on the mattress. Like she was special.

She loved this man. This was the night she'd wished for. The night she'd dreamed of for the last year. It would be the night she'd remember for the rest of her life.

"So hot." He slowly slid his hands up her thighs. Over her hips. "So freakin' hot."

No man had ever thought her *hot*.

He hooked his fingers into her briefs.

151

Her senses reeled. She lifted her hips.

He slowly slid the silk down and off her legs. "Nice." He slipped them into his pocket. His eyes smoldered. "Very nice." His voice was rough edged with want.

He leaned into her. Pressed his palms to her inner thighs. Gently pushed them open. He kissed high up on the inside of one, then the other. The scrape of his three-day-old scruff an erotic caress against her flesh. His tongue touched his lips. "I knew you'd taste like the sweetest honey."

More hot, wet heat flooded her center.

"So hot." His eyes burned her skin as they slowly slid up over her. "So sexy. All I could think about was getting my hands under that dress."

She reached for the hem bunched around her waist.

"No." His hot palm pressed against her quivering stomach. "I want to always remember you. The way you look right now."

Wariness and uncertainty snuffed some of her excitement as old insecurities took root. She leaned up on her elbows. "How do you see me?"

His finger gently slipped down over her cheek. "As the woman I can't wait to lose myself in."

Fresh desire char-broiled her uncertainty. She grabbed his wrinkled tie. Tugged him close.

He landed on top of her. Right between her legs. The hard, eager part of him pushed against her aching center. His mouth curved up into a seductive smile. "I do like me a take-charge woman."

"I do tend to go after what I want."

And she had him. Right where she wanted him.

His elbows sunk into the mattress on each side of her head. He fingered strands of her hair.

She wrapped her legs around his backside and pulled all those thick, hard inches pushing against his fly closer to her. And then she lifted her hips off the mattress. Pressed her aching center into his erection. Rubbed back and forth. And sighed out with pleasure. "You feel so good."

And then because she could, and she wanted to, she kissed him. Her fingers tunneling into his dark hair. Her tongue sliding and mating with his while his hardness pushed against her softness. An erotic hint of what was to come. And the only thing that would feel better would be him. "Naked. Inside me. Now," she told him.

He lifted his bright blue eyes to hers. And he smiled, a smile that seemed to reach inward and light him up from the inside out. It was glittering. Teasing. And breathtaking all at the same time. "Bossy, aren't we?" he teased.

And she wanted to be able to do that – to make him smile – to make him happy as he appeared to be right now for the rest of his life.

He pushed up off her.

She reached up to drag him back.

"Patience, my love." He toed off one shoe. Then the other. He hadn't worn any socks. This man who lived by a strict set of rules had a rebel soul. He wrapped his big hand around her ankle. Lifted it. His fingers teased the skin behind the ankle strap of her heel the same way he teased the skin under her shoulder strap.

And more wet heat flooded her core.

He slowly slid the ankle strap off her heel. Slipped the shoe off her foot. It dangled from one long finger.

Her size tens, dainty.

"These do amazing things to your legs." He dropped it to the floor. "But I can do amazing things, too," he told her, right before he pressed his lips to the arch of her foot and teased the sensitive skin with his tongue.

She groaned as sparks of desire spiraled up her thigh.

"You've tortured me all night." He rested her still-tingling ankle on his shoulder. "Now it's my turn." And he proceeded to her other foot. Removing her shoe and kissing her arch before resting it on his other shoulder.

"Please." She was on fire. Ready to erupt.

"Not yet, my love." He stood over her, still wearing his rumpled tuxedo jacket. His shirt was wrinkled from her hands fisting it. His tie was askew. His dark hair fell over his forehead. Hot desire burned in the depths of his blue eyes, a bright contrast to his dark beard stubble. And he looked every part, the conqueror.

She couldn't wait to be his conquest.

She slid her legs from his shoulders. Grabbed his tie and pulled herself up. She stood in front of him. "You... have too many clothes on." She unknotted his tie. Tugged it from the collar of his shirt. Dropped it to the floor. "Way too many." She slipped her hands into his jacket. The heat of his body burned her palms as she slowly slid them up over his muscled pecs.

He hissed out his pleasure. Shuffled his bulky shoulders until the garment slipped down his arms. It fell to the floor to join his tie. He reached for her dress.

"Not yet." She threw back his words.

And there was that slow, sexy smile again. And along with it, the words she'd longed to hear for a year.

"Do with me as you want."

"Oh, I will." She pulled the tails of his shirt from his trousers. Like a special Christmas present being unwrapped, ever so slowly, she slipped the buttons free. She pushed the shirt off his shoulders.

And she stared at his chest. Palmed the soft cotton of his wife-beater tee shirt. It outlined every muscle, every contour of his flat stomach. She kissed the bare skin exposed at the base of his neck. And then the skin exposed near his shoulders, before she pushed the soft cotton up his body. His stomach was flat. Hard. His pecs defined. His skin buffed and smooth. And he was, "Everything I imagined... and more."

"I know the feeling, baby." His hands slid up over her arms to the straps of her dress. "Every time I saw you tonight." His warm breath whispered against her temple. "I wanted to be the man by your side. I wanted to be the man to touch you." His tongue swirled over her earlobe.

155

Chelsea moaned.

The assault on her senses continued. His mouth hovered over the sensitive spot below her ear. "I have wanted you forever." He touched his tongue to her neck, swirling and teasing her skin there.

She palmed his shoulders to keep from melting into a puddle on the floor.

He slipped a finger under the straps of her dress. Slowly tugged them over her shoulders. And when she thought he would slide them off her arms, he stopped. "Stand there, baby. Just let me…" One finger slowly slipped into the gaping satin of her dress. Right between her breasts. Marking a trail of possession. And down further. To her stomach.

He lifted his head. His eyes, molten blue, were hot enough to singe her soul. "You are so beautiful like this. I am the luckiest man alive."

She was the lucky one.

He empowered her. His words. His actions. He made her feel things she'd never felt before with any other man.

Bold.

Beautiful.

Alluring.

"I fantasized all night about what was under this dress."

No one had ever looked at her like she was a *femme fatale*. Tonight she would be. "I guess you're gonna find out," she breathed out. She slid her fingers under the drooping straps.

Slowly slid them further down her arms, revealing a little more of her body.

"Even better, than I imagined," he rasped out with each peek. His eyes burned brighter... hotter. He wanted her. He thumbed the button on his pants. Dropped the zipper revealing an impressive tent in his boxers. His trousers slipped down his long legs. He kicked them aside and stood before. His legs were muscled. Sprinkled with dark hair. He reached for her.

The chants of the crowd gathered in the great hall matched the beat of her heart.

Ten... Nine... Eight.

The old year was coming to a close. A new one only seconds away.

Chelsea just might get her holiday wish.

Vaughn pushed his boxers down.

Oh, yeah. Her wish and a whole lot more. Answered.

He was a man in his prime, primed for her.

Seven... Six... Five.

"I want *you* naked. Now." He tossed her words back like a sexual grenade. Excitement erupted all around her. The air crackled with anticipation.

Four... Three... Two.

She slowly slid the straps off her arms. The material snagged on her breasts leaving just the tops exposed.

His breath was choppy. "I imagined you like this every time I saw you tonight."

In the grand foyer, revelers were yelling. Music was playing. Fireworks were erupting out over the Sound.

The clock on the mantel behind her struck twelve. She pushed the material off her breasts. With a little shimmy it slid off her hips, pooling on the floor at her feet. "Happy New Year, Vaughn."

Vaughn never thought he'd start the New Year with the woman he loved. Much less have her warm and willing in his arms. *Sweet, merciful Jesus.* How had he ever gotten so lucky?

He pulled her close. Sucked one nipple into his mouth. Nuzzled her breast and worked his way to the other, repeating the process. Over and over.

She responded to his every touch like no other woman. His every caress, taking her higher and higher, closer and closer to fulfillment was the hottest thing he'd ever witnessed.

He slipped between her legs. The softness of her body underneath him, the smooth silk of her skin was sexier than the glittering tease of a dress she'd worn this evening. The playful glint in her eye, and the hot wet heat he found between her legs sweeter than anything he'd ever known. He was drowning in her body. Gladly going down. She was everything he'd spent a lifetime thinking he'd never find. She was the treasure he'd never expected to unearth. She was… "Perfect," he breathed out.

He'd follow her anywhere. To the top of the highest mountain. Or the deepest hollow. She was his sun. His guiding star. He positioned his penis. Paused. Lifted his head. Touched his finger to her temple. Where it lingered. And the truth uncapped, flowed up from somewhere deep inside him. "I don't... deserve—"

She touched her finger to his lips.

He kissed them.

"There are things you need to know." Things he'd never told anyone since he'd gotten to Harrington. Things he'd thought he'd left buried in the rubble of his life in Savannah. He gently pushed a strand of hair from her cheek. "There is so much, Chelsea, you don't know—"

"Shhh." She silenced his confession.

"So much I need to say."

"No." She reached up. Touched her palms to his bristled cheeks. "You need to love me. Now."

There was no question of that. And before he could tell her what he felt for her, she tugged him closer. Gently she pressed her lips to his. And then she cocked her hips, teasing the head of his penis with her wet heat.

And then nothing mattered. Not the past. Not the mistakes he'd made. Not the purgatory he'd banished himself to for five long, regimented years. All that mattered was her.

Loving her. Pleasuring her. Spending the rest of his life with her.

Vaughn wrapped a hand around his erection, guiding it to her most sensitive spot. He slowly stroked. Back... and forth. Back... and forth. Building the anticipation. The pleasure.

She moaned. Pressed her swollen clit against his aching

cock. Torturing him as much as he was her. She panted. She gasped. He stroked faster. He added a finger. Swirled it over her swollen flesh, and she shattered in his arms.

It was the most erotically beautiful sight he'd ever seen.

She writhed. She gasped his name. Fisted the sheet in her hands as her orgasm consumed her. Fed his. And with his name still on her lips, he plunged deep inside her. The spasms of her passion gripping his penis, squeezing and pushing him closer to his own release. And the spasms came closer. And closer together as he plunged in and out of her. Faster. And faster.

Deeper.

Harder.

"More." She gasped. Grabbed his shoulders in her hands. Wrapping her legs around his waist, she lifted her hips off the bed to take him deeper.

His blood pulsed through his body. Pooling in his groin. His balls tightened as he drove both of them higher and higher, and his climax surged forward. His seed filling her the way his love for her filled his heart. And then they were both free-falling. Together. Into a blinding orgasm that rocked their bodies.

Unable to hold himself up, he rolled to one side, taking her with him. And he held her close. Their bodies still joined. Their serrated breathing mingling. Their hearts beating as one.

And for the first time in five years, Vaughn allowed peace and happiness to settle over him.

Chapter Eleven

Somewhere in the early hours of a brand new year, she'd left him.

And just when he thought he'd wake up to the woman he wanted for the rest of his life, he woke up alone. And while he'd been searching Bliss for her, worried out of his mind, she'd run from him. To his shop. And she'd left him a resignation letter. *A freakin' resignation letter!*

He banged his fist off the wall. Crushed the letter in his hand. Threw it at his desk.

He was pissed. Angry. Hurt. Every freakin' thing but happy. He sucked in a sharp breath. Dropped his head to his chest. A sigh escaped. What the hell did he do wrong? He didn't know. She wasn't around to tell him. And he was back to being pissed. Angry. Hurt.

The office door opened. He jerked his head.

Sarah peeked hers inside. "You okay?"

He pressed his lips together.

"Sorry I asked." She turned, shutting the door behind her.

He tried to breathe around the boulder of pain crushing

his chest. He was never going to be okay as long as Chelsea wasn't here. As long as she wasn't in his life. He didn't freakin' care she'd quit his business. He cared she'd walked away from *him*. That she'd walked away from everything they'd shared.

She left him.

The other office door opened. Ricky Bobby dropped a box on his desk. "I did what you told me."

"Good."

"We need to talk."

"Not now." Vaughn had things to put in order. Things to take care of before he could chase after her. It had been two freakin', interminably long days since he'd woke up without her. It wasn't going to turn into three.

"*Yes, now.* The boys and I are putting you on notice."

"Nobody *puts me on notice.* I'm the boss."

"You just think you are. Everybody knows Cha-Cha is the heart and soul of this place."

He didn't want to talk about hearts. Or souls. "I gave you orders. I expect them to be followed."

"Do I look like an idiot?"

"No." Vaughn was the idiot.

"Just get her back here. Do not let the best thing to ever happen to you get away."

There was a chorus of agreement from Michelangelo, Re-Pete, Josh, and Shakespeare. They were all wedged in the doorway behind Ricky Bobby.

"So, I guess…" Vaughn took his first bite of crow. "Everybody in the shop knows?"

"That you got the hots for Cha-Cha? That you've had them for like ever. Yeah, pretty much," his third in command replied.

"Go after her." This from Sarah. "Apologize."

"I didn't do anything wrong! *She left me.*"

"You're a man."

"What the hell's that supposed to mean?"

"It means, boss." Ricky Bobby pushed the box of *No Employee Dating* signs closer. The corners were bent and dented from being pried off the walls. "That you'll do what's right. You always do."

And weren't those the words he'd waited five years to hear.

* * *

There was no place like home. But even home couldn't mend what was broken inside. And two days, or two hundred wasn't going to change that. Yet Chelsea needed to be here. In the sturdy log home with the green tin roof nestled on the side of Carter Mountain in Harlan County, Kentucky. She needed to figure out where she went from here.

Or decide if *here* was where she would stay.

She could work with her papa again making furniture. She could—

"Don't get me wrong, Chelsea Sophia. It's real nice havin'

you here, but shouldn't you be at work?"

Her papa wasn't letting up. He'd been asking some variation of that same question for the last two days.

Head down, she kept chopping. Carrots. Celery. Potatoes. Onion. It would all go into a pot. With a few other ingredients and time simmering over a gas flame, it would turn into a thick, nourishing vegetable beef soup. Perfect to ward off the twenty-five degree blustery cold that was swirling around outside. But not even her mother's prized recipe could mend her broken heart. Or warm her soul.

"You quit, didn't you?"

She reached for the two-inch thick slab of beef. "Merle dropped this off earlier. He butchered yesterday. It doesn't get much fresher." She methodically sliced the meat into small, bite-sized cubes. She didn't answer her papa. Fervently hoped he'd forget.

"You quit, didn't you?" he asked again. "And just so you know, you don't have the market cornered on stubborn, child. I'll keep askin' until you answer me. You quit, didn't you?"

"Yes!" She slammed the knife down on the granite counter. Unclenched her fisted hand. "Yes, I quit." A thin mask of civility barely covered her churning emotions. She picked up the knife. Grabbed a few more vegetables and tried to regain control while the sharp steel blade sliced through a crisp red potato.

"Why?" He stepped closer. Leaned a hip against the counter, and she was glad she'd left her hair loose. It concealed one side of her face. He lifted it to better see. "You loved that job."

She wiped the corner of her eye with the back of her hand. Silently blamed the onions for the watery tears that had been falling since that unforgettable night at Bliss.

"Why, Chelsea?"

She lifted her head. Wearily replied, "I made a mistake, okay?" A big one. One she couldn't talk to him about. He hadn't wanted to talk about boys when she was sixteen. Or periods. Or makeup. He surely wouldn't want to talk about her fixing her hair, getting all made up, and sleeping with her boss on New Year's Eve.

And neither did she.

She swiped the back of her hand against the side of her face. *Damn onions.*

He carefully tucked the chunk of hair behind her ear. The rough pad of his thumb gently rubbed against her wet cheek. "You couldn'ta done anything so bad as to warrant tears."

She hadn't cried since her mother had died.

But she'd surely cried her share and more in the last few days.

She looked into his concerned eyes as more tears filled hers. "Oh, Papa. I did."

She didn't want to think how she'd poached on another woman's date. Or how she'd taken what she'd wanted, fully aware he was hurting. Shame and remorse filled her. She took something that wasn't hers to take.

165

All because she'd wanted him.

And she didn't want to think about him either. How he'd kept his distance when she'd thrown herself at him before. But one night dressed up and he was sleeping with her. Having sex with her because of how she looked. Seeing her only as a desirable woman when she donned a dress and heels.

She looked through the small window over the sink to the snow-covered yard and the mountain beyond. A few flakes were still falling. Shadows of twilight were slowly creeping up out of the hollow, snuffing out the fading daylight. Soon it would be dark. And she will have made it through another day. She tried not to think about how bleak, how barren her life was going to be without him in it.

More bleak, more barren than this snow-covered mountain in January. She rubbed the pinch in her chest. Her heart was broken. Her soul mortally wounded.

"You can't do bad, chil'." Papa rubbed his finger against her wet cheek again. She looked up. In his eyes she saw the paternal love she'd come to depend on. "You're a Chathford. You do stubborn."

One corner of her trembling mouth curled up. If he could ignore the six-foot-six, sinfully handsome elephant in the room, the one with the piercing blue eyes and ever-present three-day scruff on his jaw, so could she. She stepped into her papa's embrace.

Just like he'd done when she'd been sixteen, he wrapped his big arms around her and hugged her. And she sucked it up. Stubbornly willed the tears to stop. She knew he hated them.

Because they reminded him Sophia Chathford was no longer in this kitchen, rubbing her hands on a tea towel before pulling her girl child aside and taking care of those *womanly things* he'd been left to handle with his wife's passing.

I miss you, Momma.

She pulled back out of his arms. Managed a weak smile. Even kept her voice from wobbling when she said, "I better get this soup on. So we can eat before midnight."

He nodded.

And with or without Garrett Vaughn Jennings the Third, her life would go on.

* * *

Chelsea was setting the table when the unmistakable rumble of a heavy duty Ford pickup truck swept up through the hollow. She dropped the bowls with a clatter. Her heart knocked against her chest.

Papa looked over. Concern drew his brows together. "You expectin' someone?"

She jerked her head side to side.

He walked to the oak door and opened it. Stepped out onto the snow-dusted porch.

Grabbing her jacket, she quickly followed. A jumbled prayer of *please let it be* and *please no* fervently falling from her lips.

The *please let it be* plea was granted. And she didn't know what to do.

She knew that truck. She'd driven in it for five years. Had kissed a man senseless in it, too. She rubbed her fingers under her eyes. She'd cried enough today her mascara was pooled there like dark circles of an all-nighter.

The truck stopped. The driver's side door opened. A scuffed, size fifteen work boot appeared. Then a long jean-covered leg. Vaughn stepped down.

"*No.*" Her heart spasmed. "No," she whispered again. She followed her papa like his prized hunting dog off the porch down the stone walk.

Nothing could prepare her for seeing him. Here. Looking haggard. And determined. And—

Her heart beat harder in her chest, stumbling all over the debris of hope and joy and hurt. That damn hurt.

"Chelsea? You know this man?"

Of course, she did. She worked for him. She loved him. She slept with him. And she'd ran away from him. She managed a mute nod.

"Introduce us," he softly reprimanded her.

And while she rubbed her chest, she stuttered out introductions. "Garrett Vaughn Jennings the Third, my father. Ellsworth Chathford."

Vaughn stepped forward. "Nice to meet you, sir." He offered his hand.

Papa shook it.

Vaughn turned toward her. And the mask of civility fell

away. His blue eyes were blazing. Probing. Turbulent. Demanding. "We need to talk."

"You can talk inside." Papa lifted an arm toward the front door.

"No!" Was he crazy? She wanted this man gone. Gone before she did something foolish. And feminine. Like cry in front of him.

"Chelsea! Invite the man in. He drove all the way up here."

"Well, he can just drive all the way back down!" He was *not* coming inside her house.

"Chelsea Sophia." Papa's bushy gray brows drew down over his blue eyes. "Where's your Christian charity?"

"Did you not hear me? I don't wanna talk to him!"

"Well, I'm not leaving until we do."

She turned. Glared at the man who'd broken her heart. "Fine. Then you stay. I'll leave."

She hadn't gotten two steps away from him. He took her elbow. Slowly turned her toward him. "Why did you leave? Me?" His voice was hoarse. Filled with pain she hadn't expected.

"I'm not having this conversation." Especially with her papa standing near. She pulled her arm free.

"Chelsea!" he called out again. He moved toward her. She pushed him away. Before he, or her father could stop her, she broke into a run.

"Chelsea!" Vaughn yelled, helplessly watching the woman

he loved run away from him for the second time in two days. "Get back here. Please! I wanna talk to you!"

"You can bark all the orders you want, son." Ellsworth Chathford stepped closer. "But that dog won't hunt."

Vaughn turned to the big man standing beside him.

"She's a Chathford. She's a might stubborn. And she is only gonna heel when *she* wants to heel." The man turned. Lifted his hand toward the oak door with the oval etched glass. "You might as well come inside. Sit a spell."

"Thank you. But I'll wait here."

Ellsworth eyed him. "I see stubborn has already met stubborn. Suit yourself." He paused at the front door. "Just one more thing, son." He turned back to Vaughn. "If I find out you're the cause for any more of my daughter's tears, all that Christian charity bullshit talk is out the window."

Vaughn could look Ellsworth in the eye. They were the same height. But Ellsworth was broader, thicker through the chest and arms. There was no doubt he'd kick Vaughn's ass into next week. "I have no intention of hurting your daughter. I'd like permission to court her."

Ellsworth's brows drew down. So did his mouth. "Chelsea's a full-grown woman. She can make her own choices."

"Yes, she can." She'd made the choice to leave him, hadn't she? "I'm still asking permission, sir."

"That's a little… unusual."

"It's old fashioned, but Chelsea's very special to me." He'd never met anyone like her.

"And you want permission to court her."

"Yes, sir. I do." He wanted a hell of a lot more. But that was a start.

Ellsworth smiled. "You know, son." He nodded his head. "There might still be hope for you yet."

Vaughn didn't hold out much hope. He'd been standing on the front porch for forty-five minutes, freezing his ass off, waiting for the most stubborn woman on the planet to cool down and come back. Just when he was ready to give up and head back down off this damnable mountain before night swallowed it, he saw a curvaceous blond slowly making her way down a steep path.

He met her near one of the outbuildings. He'd startled her. She sucked in a sharp breath. Her cheeks were chapped red from the wind. Her eyes were red, too, from tears. Tears he'd caused. Helplessly, he stood in front of her. "I'm sorry, Chelsea. For whatever I did, I am so sorry."

Chelsea hadn't expected him to still be here. Hadn't expected to have to confront what she'd been avoiding. Her guilt. "It's not yours to be sorry," she softly said.

His dark brows furrowed over his blue eyes. The corners of his mouth pulled down.

"I took something that wasn't mine." She rubbed a finger under her eye. "I wanted you. And I... I took what I wanted." She dropped her gaze. "You were with Sydney." She swallowed. "And I— I just—"

171

Vaughn cussed. "You think I just rolled over and had sex with you? Give me a little freakin' credit, will you?"

"You don't get it, do you?" His anger fueled hers. "You only had sex with me because of how I looked!" There she'd said it.

A red flush of anger crawled up over his tensed jaw.

"Admit it! I threw myself at you and you always turned me away. But—"

"You think because you had a freakin' dress on I couldn't control myself?"

It sounded so ridiculous when he said it but, "yes," she softly replied.

He was shaking his head slowly side to side. "No." His voice was soft. "You are so wrong, sweetheart." So certain. He stepped closer. Into her space. Making her feel all kinds of crazy things. Snow fell harder around them. Clinging to the dark strands of his hair, dusting his shoulders. He lifted his hand. Gently touched her hair. "I have loved you for a long, long time."

The breath backed up in Chelsea's lungs. Oh how she wanted to believe. But… "No, you haven't."

"Your dad was right. Stubborn to a fault." His mouth curled up. Just a small smile, but it erased years of strain from his face. And she wanted to believe so badly.

"You were beautiful in that dress. I'm not gonna lie to you. But I think you're freakin' hot when you wear that royal blue Henley."

She pressed her palm to her chest. So afraid to believe. So afraid to hope.

His finger slid to her cheek. "It matches your eyes."

She knew the one. But that he'd noticed that detail? Surprise and cautious joy filled her.

"The one that shows off every beautiful curve," he added, as his hands settled on hips she'd always thought a little too big. "The one you wear on alternating Tuesdays and Thursdays."

She pressed her palm over her fluttering heart.

He dropped his hold. A seriousness she had never seen settled over his face. "When I came to Harrington, Chels, I was broken. I didn't know shit about restoring anything."

"You knew exactly what you were doing. I was in awe of all you had planned."

Again he shook his head side to side. "I was like a cheap veneer, sweetheart. I looked good on the outside. But I had nothing of value inside. But you." His finger slowly slid down her cheek. "You were the real thing, honey. A perfect original."

"I don't understand." None of this made sense.

"I came here from Savannah. After I buried my father."

"I'm sorry, Vaughn." She knew how painful losing a parent was.

"It was my fault. All my fault." He leaned against the wall. Dropped his head back. Squeezed his eyes shut. As if the weight of his confession was too much to bear.

"I destroyed my father's company. The one my grandfather had started."

The words came haltingly slow. Like they were pulled from deep in his wounded soul.

"All because I got involved with a woman at work." He rubbed the heels of his palms into his eyes.

She stepped closer. Touched her fingertips to his temple. "I'm so sorry."

He dropped his gaze, as if ashamed. "My father tried to warn me. But I didn't listen. I was so hot for her. She did everything I wanted. And things," he huffed out a self-deprecating breath. Slowly shook his head side to side. "Things I could only imagine."

"I..." She didn't want to hear this.

He lifted his head. "But she didn't care about me. Not the way I thought she did."

"You loved her?"

He didn't confirm. Or deny. *He loved her.* She knew he had.

"She used me, Chels. To sabotage Jennings Antiquities. And because I couldn't see that, even when it was pointed out—" He lifted a broad shoulder. "I destroyed our company. And the stress..." He swallowed. "It killed my father." His voice was hoarse, wavering with pain. "I killed my father."

"No." Chelsea slid her palm against the base of his head. She pulled him close, their foreheads touching. She pressed a kiss to his throat, his skin cold from the biting wind. "You made a mistake. You're not perfect. You're human."

He lifted his head. "How could I not love you?" He gently brushed his fingers against her cheek. "You always see me in the best of light. There was no thinking. I definitely destroyed the family business. And the stress from that caused the heart attack that killed my father."

"Vaughn." She touched his wind-reddened cheeks with her palms. "You don't know that."

"I tried, Chelsea. I tried really hard. For four years. But this last year, I couldn't look anywhere else. It was you I wanted. But all I had was that dumb rule. My stupid way of trying to make up to my father for my mistake."

"Honey, there is no making up when—"

"I know that. All I can do now is learn from my mistakes. And live my life the best I can." He took her hand. Turned them toward his truck. "I have something for you."

"Isn't the confession enough?" she asked, walking with him.

"Not near enough." He reached behind the seat. Pulled out a cardboard box. He handed it to her.

The flaps were hastily tucked under each other. It was wrapped with twine, the edges fashioned into a simple bow. She lifted her eyes to his.

"Open it."

She looked down. Gently tugged the string. Pulled up the flaps of the box. It was filled with the *no employee dating* signs from the shop. She lifted her eyes to his. "Your rule."

"Duly rescinded and reversed. No rule is more important than you."

Her mouth trembled.

"I apologized to Josh and Sarah like you told me. I gave them their jobs back, too. With promotions."

Her trembling lips formed a wobbly smile.

"I fell in love with a beautiful woman who came into my shop in the darkest time of my life. You made it bearable. You made me believe again. In myself. And in love. I don't care what you wear, honey. Or what you look like. My heart and my soul fell in love with yours."

"I—" Tears of happiness filled her eyes. "We," her heart and her soul, "love you, too," she whispered.

* * *

Clutching the box of signs to her chest, Chelsea and Vaughn walked back to the cabin. Inside, they stole a long steamy kiss under the mistletoe in the entryway.

"So, Chelsea Sophia, I, uh, see you decided to let our guest spend the night."

Her father was sitting by a warm, welcoming fire in his favorite chair, a book in his hand. "Yes, Papa. Vaughn is spending the night."

With a palm to the base of her spine, Vaughn gently walked them further into the living room. "I'd like permission to marry your daughter, sir."

Papa rose from his chair. "First, you wanna court? Now

you wanna marry?" Papa turned his head to her.

She held out the box of bent-up signs. "I love him, Papa."

Her papa's brow wrinkled as he stared down at the box she held out to him. He looked over at Vaughn still standing so stiff and straight by her side, awaiting a reply.

"You know, in my day, son." He patted Vaughn's shoulder. "When we asked a woman to marry, we gave her a ring. Not a box of old signs."

Chapter Twelve

Vaughn bought Chelsea a ring.

Six weeks later, on February fourteenth, the holiday dedicated to love, he waited at the base of the grand staircase in Bliss, the home his company had restored not once – but twice. He was surrounded by a close-knit circle of friends. Bobby Wayne and Lauren Forsythe. Josh and Sarah. The numb-nuts from the shop. And a rather large contingent of Chelsea's family and friends who'd traveled in from Harlan County.

The room was filled with roses. Their sweet fragrance mingled with the scent of vanilla from the candles that illuminated the foyer with golden light. But it paled in comparison to the beautiful woman standing at the top of the staircase.

Rays of sunshine filtering in from the cathedral windows high above spilled over her, catching in her golden hair. It rippled down over her hourglass figure, bathing her in a fountain of light, before cascading down the long staircase like Nature's footman rolling out a golden carpet for her descent.

Anticipation pulsed through his veins. She loved him. Had agreed to marry him.

With the chords of a familiar strain, the pianist announced to those gathered the bride had arrived. Guests turned. The hall filled with hushed excitement as the woman he loved gracefully moved to the top step.

His heart overflowed with love as his beautiful bride slowly walked down the towering column of marble and mahogany on the arm of her father. True to her love of history, she wore the off-the-shoulder gown her momma had worn when Sophia Chathford had married Ellsworth. And as always, when she smiled at him, his soul sighed out with peace and contentment.

She made him happy.

He was a better man for knowing her. He loved her. He always would. And she would always know that. Those were his silent vows to her.

Father and daughter descended the steps. While the music crescendoed all around them, they slowly walked through the crowd. The music stopped. Ellsworth kissed his daughter before slipping her arm from his. He offered it to Vaughn. "Take good care of her, son."

"I plan to, sir," Vaughn solemnly replied. He intended to make her blissfully happy for the rest of their lives. And while the minister who'd traveled from the Church of Christ in Cumberland, Kentucky officiated, Vaughn and Chelsea their vows.

Gently, Vaughn took Chelsea's hand. "You're the joy in my heart. And the peace in my soul and I will love you for the rest of my life."

Chelsea's beautiful lips, shining with gloss, curved up. "I love you, Vaughn. And I will love you forever."

Vaughn bent his head. And he kissed her. He lifted his head. Gazed into her beautiful eyes. "I lived my life. Every step… every mistake, every decision to get me here. To you."

Her eyes were dewy soft with love. "You restored my faith. You refinished my story. And you are rewriting my future."

"It's you." He touched her cheek. "You who have made me new. You scraped away the flaws of my past. With your love," he swallowed. "You've given me a future. One I vow to spend with your for the rest of my life."

They shared their first official kiss as husband and wife.

And while they signed their marriage license and incorporation papers – his company was now Chathford-Jennings Restoration – Lauren directed the guests to the main dining room.

There they ate. They toasted. They kissed some more. And with their hands clasped together and their heads ducked low, Vaughn and Chelsea ran through the gauntlet of well-wishers gathered on both sides of the main entrance of the stately old mansion. The exuberant group eagerly showered them with bubbles and bird seed as they ran to their awaiting limo.

The car pulled away, leaving the strains of whistles and cheers a sigh on the evening breeze. "Our hosts definitely know how to party." Vaughn opened the bottle of Jim Beam Bobby Wayne and Lauren had stashed in the car.

"They do." Chelsea fidgeted with the front of her gown. "I think I have birdseed in my bra."

"I can take care of that for you." Vaughn handed her a glass.

Chelsea took it. "I'm sure you can. And you will."

Vaughn clinked his glass against hers, taking a sip. And while Chelsea took a sip from hers, his fingers slipped down the front of her gown. She sat the glass aside as he kissed her neck and ear.

"A little eager, are we?" she teased, taking his glass.

He slipped his hand under her gown. "Nothing little about me." His palm slowly slid up her calf, up over her knee, and further up her thigh.

"And don't I know that." she wholeheartedly agreed while her own hands slowly slid up his leg to his groin. She leaned into him, her lips touching his. Her tongue slipped into his mouth as the limo turned onto the main boulevard leading to town, leaving the shell driveway of Bliss behind.

Metal banged against metal and asphalt.

"Sorry, sir." A disembodied voice came over the intercom. "I need to pull over."

Vaughn slipped his fingers out from the silk of her panties as the limo pulled to the side of the road.

Chelsea straightened her gown.

With a quick kiss, and a muttered cuss, he opened the back door. Stepped out. Followed the limo driver to the back of the car.

Chelsea followed him, trying hard to hide a smile.

Attached to the bumper with twine were a dozen *No Employee Dating* signs.

Vaughn stared down at the scratched and dented metal. "My rule?" He lifted his head. Looked at her, his lips twitching. "The numb nuts? Or you?"

She didn't confirm. Or deny. Just shrugged a shoulder. "Seemed a fitting place for them."

"Wanna know another fitting place?" He toed one of the signs before pulling her into his arms. "You." He dipped his head. "In my heart. Forever."

"Then wishes really do come true," she whispered, pressing her lips to his.

Especially a holiday wish.

A Note from the Author

I hope you enjoyed reading Vaughn and Chelsea's story as much as I did writing it. I had lots of fun going back to Harrington, visiting with old friends at Bliss. If I've "revved" your curiosity and you want more, you can find Lauren and Bobby Wayne's story told in *Beyond the Checkered Flag*.

Did you like *Holiday Wish*? Let everyone know by posting a review at **www.amazon.com**. It really is the best way a writer can be promoted.

And now a little more about me, the author.

I have always loved a happy ending. And dreams that come true. I love weaving tales where the boy gets his girl, and they find all their dreams come true as they live happily ever after. That's how it is in the Land of "Wylde".

A misplaced mountain child, I live in the rolling hills of Western Pennsylvania with my husband of more than thirty-five years. (My very own restorer of lost dreams. How cool is that!) Together we have raised three handsome sons. There was never a dull moment at our house. It was the house that testosterone built.

Please visit me at my website **www.jdwylde.com**. Become a member of the Wylde nation by "liking" my fan page on Facebook (j.d. wylde) where you can keep up to date on all things "Wylde". You can follow me on Twitter, too, @jdwylde.

I look forward to hearing from you. And as always... *live Wylde* !

Other Books by J.D. Wylde

Sweet Romances

The Journey

The Dream

Mainstream Contemporary Romances – Sexy!

When Push Comes to Shove

When Law Met Disorder

Karma in Camo

Cupid in Camo

Bliss: An Anthology of Novellas

Beyond the Checkered Flag (single release)

Holiday Bliss

22382265R00108

Made in the USA
Middletown, DE
29 July 2015